A VEXING VALENTINE

A STANDALONE HOLIDAY PARANORMAL ROMANCE

MONSTERS OF THE DIVIDE
BOOK 2

T. B. WIESE

1-13372385031

This is a work of fiction. Names, characters, places, and incidents either are the product of the author's imagination or are used fictitiously. Any resemblance to actual persons, living or dead, events, or locales is entirely coincidental.

Cover design by GetCovers

Chapter art by T. B. Wiese in Canva Pro

ISBN: 978-1-959657-12-5 ebook

ISBN: 978-1-959657-13-2 paperback

OTHER BOOKS IN THIS WORLD

- Paine for the Holidays
- A Vexing Valentines
- A Malicious Summer Vacation (coming summer 2024)
- Hunted on Halloween (coming fall 2024)

Hold onto the good things

AUTHOR'S NOTE

**Please take care of yourself and your mental health

A Vexing Valentine is an ADULT paranormal romance that contains elements such as: monsters, violence, swearing, blood, gore, use of weapons including guns and knives, biting, claiming, mention of religious holidays, loss of a loved one, and sexually explicit scenes ... with monsters.

MONSTERS OF THE DIVIDE

*Most of these are only briefly mentioned in passing, so don't feel too overwhelmed.

Dremar (Our MMC) - *Think vampire and gargoyle. This species has different colored skin. Our MMC has blue-grey skin that is smooth and hairless, but others have shades of red or green or black ... Eyes to match their skin color. Males and females have curly horns like an antelope. They are very fast on foot, even faster when flying. They have bat-like wings, a snake-like tail, fangs, and claws. They drink blood, not to survive, but to obtain power. They heal very quickly. Any being that they've tasted the blood of, they can incinerate with a thought. The dremar, but especially our MMC, are feared by other monsters.*

Xani - *Scaled skin that is very tough. Hairless. Usually green but can be other colors. They have reflective, reptile-like eyes. Sharp teeth. Extremely fast. Can walk upright or on all fours. They have snake-like tails, and hate the light, always sticking to shadows unless the hunt of a prey brings them out.*

Joteunn - *Fur-covered like a werewolf, only they don't shift. They have wolf-like ears and a snout with sharp teeth and fangs. They are pretty large comparatively in the monster world and are extremely strong. They heal very quickly as long as they have the magic to do so. They occasionally run in packs but prefer to hunt solo (as most monsters do). They do howl and bark to communicate, though they also speak.*

Grateslung - *Snake-like creature with the bottom half of a snake, the top half looks like a gargoyle without wings. Stone-like skin on the body, scaled skin on the lower half. Usually shades of grey or black but can be different colors. Their saliva is venomous, and they are very strong and fast.*

Quilen - *Tall, humanoid monster that's thin but muscled. They have branch-like horns that look too heavy to hold up. They are dark skinned with black eyes, long spindly fingers with claws. They aren't the fastest of monsters, but they are strong and can slip between shadows.*

Grae - *Feathered all over. Humanoid body with a sharp beak, eagle talons for feet, and wings for arms. They are not the smartest monster - they are more animalistic.*

Nepha - *Humanoid with metallic feathered wings. These are the creatures Angles were modeled from. They are exceptional hunters - even our MMC is wary of them. They are beautiful but cruel. Most believe that if they have hearts, they are made of stone.*

Hellhounds - *Large dog-like creatures the size of a pony. They do not speak. They hunt in packs, but once their prey is caught, it's every hellhound for themselves. They are a little further down on the food chain in the monster realm, which is why they tend to stay in groups.*

Anza - *Smaller comparatively in the monster realm - about the size of the average human female. They have shimmery skin like starlight. They are pretty and disarming. They are one of the fastest monsters, able to move so quickly they are a blur. They have sharp teeth, a hypnotizing gaze, and can secrete hallucinogens from their skin to incapacitate their prey, which they like to peel and eat. Death by anza is very slow and painful. Not only can they heal themselves, but they can heal others - if you can convince them to.*

Unicorns - *They look just like our myths. Horse-like creatures with a single horn. But these unicorns are carnivorous with serrated teeth, razor sharp hooves, and are so strong, they can cave in a monster's chest with one kick. Their horns also emit a strong electric shock that can incapacitate or even kill.*

Menace - spider like monsters with blades for legs. Hairy. Can't see well. Relies on sound waves and sense of smell. They lay eggs like spiders and shoot webs.

We might meet more monsters in the upcoming books in this series, but these are all the ones in this story.

Enjoy.

CHAPTER 1

THE SIXTY SECONDS THAT CHANGED THE WORLD

Monsters are real.

Seventy-two years ago, they came.

Supposedly, at first, everyone thought it was a hoax. But it didn't take long for the world to realize that what was happening was indeed real. You can still find old clips of videos people took on their phones that night.

The monsters came through what we now call The Divide—the invisible barrier that separated our realm from theirs. Apparently, all throughout history, the occasional monster would get through—those folktales of werewolves, vampires, and fae started from somewhere. But that night, they all just ... appeared. So many humans lost their lives. The monsters took what they wanted ... blood, bones, fear, souls. Weapons didn't work on most of them ... with their tough skin, scales, super speed, wings, regenerative healing ... The humans were no match. It was a bloodbath. Then, six hours after they appeared, they all just vanished.

The entire planet was still reeling from the attack when it happened the next night, and the next. Always at the same time. Always for six hours. It wasn't until almost a week of the occurrences that someone discovered that the first night the monsters came through, all time stood still for one full minute. Clocks ceased ticking, tides froze, the world stopped turning. No one noticed, because well, monsters. And no one really knows how life on earth survived the literal freezing of time. Time hasn't stopped again since that first night, but the monsters still come.

Humanity's saving grace came with the discovery of magic symbols with the power to keep the monsters out. Who discovered it? That truth is buried under wild conjectures, outlandish legends, and fantastical myths. So, who knows?

And here we are. Life goes on. We go about the monster-free hours almost as normally as before, as if we're trying to ignore the nightmare we know is coming with the fall of The Divide every day. But we all know ...

The monsters *are* coming, and if you want to survive, there are only three rules:

Make sure the correct symbols are carved deep into your threshold and every windowsill.

Be sure you recharge the symbols with a few drops of your blood at least once a month to keep the monsters out.

And whatever you do, don't go outside after the final curfew siren.

CHAPTER 2

MAX

"Come on, Max, let me stay the night."

Shoving my hands in my pockets, I fight to keep from rolling my eyes. How many times are we going to have this argument? Peter stares at me with what he would call his puppy dog expression, but the wide, sad eyes and pouty lip just annoy me. He runs his hands through his short brown hair, obviously flexing with the movement.

Ugh.

Cracking my knuckles, I say, "Peter, I—"

"No. No." He throws up his hands, his innocent look melting away, replaced with annoyance. "You know what? I'm tired of this. We've been dating for a month, and you still refuse to let me add my blood to your thresholds."

A month? Has it been that long?

He rolls his eyes, his face flushing as he goes on. "I've

offered to let you stay at my place, but you always turn me down. I'm not going to waste my time if you're going to refuse to let me in."

I get the feeling he means more than my townhouse. I guess I understand, but *it's* just not there between us. Surely, he feels there's something missing. I'm not willing to settle in a relationship. He shouldn't either. I get it. It's hard out there these days ...

The memory of Reece's blue eyes flash in my mind, his crooked smile haunting my memories. My breath stutters. I can picture him so clearly; I can almost smell the woodsy scent of his deodorant. Swallowing, I force his memory away, but the pain digs at me, like he's dying all over again.

A gasp nearly escapes my lips as the chasm of despair opens under me, threatening to pull me into its darkness. It's been over ten years, and I've worked hard to climb out of the depthless well of sadness, but sometimes I'm blindsided. Like now.

I realize Peter has gone silent. I press my thumb to each of my fingers, trying to crack my knuckles again, but I get no such reprieve. Peter's sigh has me meeting his gaze. I know this is my fault. I should feel bad, but ... I'm relieved. He's going to leave me. Now I don't have to be the one to break it off.

Without a word, Peter turns, heading for the door, his footfalls quiet but dragging. Despite knowing we're not right for each other, there's a pang in my chest. No one enjoys being alone. I'm no exception ... especially with Valentine's Day a week away.

I'm a big guy, and Peter calls me stoic which I know is double speak for unapproachable. But Reece used to say I'm a secret romantic. And he was right, when it came to him anyway. I haven't found anything even close to what we had since he ... when that monster ...

With his hand on the doorknob, Peter bows his head. "Take care of yourself, Max."

I'm surprised at the emotion in my voice as I say, "You too, Peter."

His fingers tighten on the handle before he yanks open the door and leaves, quickly taking the steps down to the sidewalk. His sports car rumbles to life. I hate that car. It's too flashy, too loud. As he pulls away from the curb, the car roars, and I grit my teeth. I would never drive something like that. I may be retired from my old life, but my modified SUV still sits in my single-car garage around back. It is one of the few things I've kept from my monster hunter days; the vehicle, my favorite weapons, and the painting. I haven't taken the SUV out since ...

Well, the last time I climbed into the driver's seat, I ended up losing track of time, and before I realized it, the Divide was about to fall. The monsters were coming. I took a turn too fast in my rush to get home, and a spent shell rolled out from under the passenger seat. Reece and I were always good about cleaning up after a hunt, so who knows where that bullet casing was lodged for all those years? The sight of it sent me spiraling into a memory as I sped through the streets. It was like Reece was sitting right there next to me, leaning out the window to fire his rifle at a pack of monsters. The image was so vividly clear, I could smell the gunpowder and feel the breeze.

I was so lost in the flashback, I clipped the curb as I turned onto my street, and the brass casing rolled back under the seat. Tears blurred my vision, and I nearly crashed into the back wall of my garage as the anger, depression, agony, and sadness flooded me. I wanted to rush back out into the night, killing monsters until I met my own end. I wanted blood and violence. I wanted revenge. But instead, I spent nearly an hour just staring blankly at the steering wheel, hands gripping the leather tightly as I tried to catch my breath. I don't even remember if I picked up the casing. It's probably still there.

No. The SUV will stay in my garage. I've gotten used to walking or taking public transportation.

As the grating sound of Peter's car fades, I press my hands to the door jam. My gaze travels across the street. Something has been going on over there. During the Christmas holidays, there were so many monsters hunting and fighting, it was like they were all drawn to this street. But then, after the new year, it quieted down significantly.

Now, it's almost like the monsters are too scared to venture down this street. And if they do, they rush by, glances flicking towards the blue townhouse. But also, since the holidays, *it* has been showing up. Every night. For weeks.

I shake off my unease as best I can, staring at the front door across the street. I've enjoyed the relative quiet since Christmas, so I don't poke my nose where it doesn't belong. Closing my door, the soft click seems to echo in my empty house. I need a distraction.

A long, hot shower relaxes me slightly, but I'm shocked at the few tears that escape my burning eyes to mix with the water. I'm not mourning my relationship with Peter, not really. I'm just tired and ... lonely. I've always loved Valentine's Day. Reece and I used to ...

The shower is no longer helping. Getting out, I hastily dry off, feeling patches of wet skin on my back as I pull on a worn t-shirt and drawstring sweatpants. I stuff my socked feet into my well broken-in boots. Moving silently around my townhouse, I turn off all the lights, fighting against the dread that threatens to freeze me in place. Even after all these years, I still hate the dark.

Forcing myself to move silently through the shadows of my house, I check each hidden place that holds my weapons. Before heading to the kitchen at the back of my house, I stop at the long table in the front hall. I glare at the painting hanging on the wall, a Valentine's gift from Reece. The little red riding hood scene is dark, the tree branches reaching for a lone figure walking down the middle of the path. Glowing eyes stare from the shadows, watching the figure. But instead of a little girl in a red cape, my broad back stalks through the woods, my kit secured, gun in hand, ready to face the monsters. In the painting, my shirt is red, a color I'd never wear on a hunt, but Reece really leaned into the little red riding hood theme.

I've almost thrown this painting out dozens of times while in the depths of my despair, but I never did. I never will.

I pull the edge of the frame, and the painting swings away from the wall. I enter the code, a green light flashes, and I open the safe. Bypassing two of Reece's pistols, I grab the box of ammo, counting out fifteen bullets. I also pick up my small holster before closing and locking the safe. I slide the painting back in place without looking at it.

The bullets clink in my large hand as I silently stride to the kitchen. I grab the back of a chair, lifting it so it doesn't scrape on the wood floor. Setting it down by the window, I take a seat. The chair groans softly as I lean to the side, opening a lower cabinet door. Reaching, I find the small metal box that's secured to the back inside wall. Using muscle memory, I easily find the little pad that reads my fingerprint, and a soft click sounds. My palm wraps around the custom grip of my gun, then I close the lockbox with the back of my hand and wait for the same little click sound as it locks.

Setting the ammo, holster, and pistol on the counter, I glance at the thick book sitting there, the pages worn, a burn mark on one edge, a scratch down the plain black cover. Flipping it open, it falls right to the page I've been studying for the past few weeks.

There are many monsters documented in this book. Reece and I and the others in our hunter squad spent years recording the monsters. If we found weaknesses, they were documented in this book. Reece drew the little sketch at the top of this particular page. He was much more talented than me at capturing the monsters' likenesses, but I've added a lot to this page since New Year's. My notes and inferior sketches nearly fill the space.

I've been watching the monster that has been watching me, and tonight I'm going to make my move.

Peeling my gaze from the book, I shift to find a comfortable position as I look out the window. Running a hand through my blond hair, I slick back the damp strands before moving my fingers in the practiced move of loading my magazine. It's almost like a meditation as each round slides into place. When I'm done, I check the safety and rest the pistol in my lap.

I breathe in, hold it, and slowly let it out. Over and over, I pace my breaths, sinking into the headspace of my hunter mode. I wait. I know the monster is coming. It always comes. Does it realize I've been watching it?

The first warning siren goes off, and my skin tingles.

The Divide is about to fall. I lean back, forcing myself to relax, though what I really want to do is lean forward and flick on a light—to banish the shadows and let the monster see me tonight.

The second siren blares outside as the automated voice says, "One minute until The Divide breach." I clench my fists. I'm feeling reckless tonight, and if Reece were here, he'd chastise me with that husky chuckle that always had me melting for him.

The final warning goes off. The Divide is down. The monsters are free to roam our realm, all too eager to hunt and kill any human stupid enough to be outside the protection of their blood-carvings.

Angrily, I rub at the pain in my chest. So many of my old hunter team are gone. Dead. Some still meet up and hunt, trying to fight back ... fighting the monsters, fighting the hopelessness. I look down at the small x's tattooed on my arm. They start on the back of my wrist and climb towards my elbow. So many. One for each monster kill. Sometimes I miss my hunter days. I miss the chase, the satisfaction of watching another monster die by my hand. But I got out of that life after Reece ...

I'm feeling caged in tonight. The old familiar fight instinct flares to life inside me, making everything sharp and clear. Just as it has done almost every night since Christmas, the monster appears with a slight shifting of the shadows in the street. I slide my holster inside my waistband, securing it before my hand curls around the comforting grip of my gun.

The monster is hard to see where it's tucked into the shadows, but I know what it looks like. Its skin is so dark it easily blends into the night. It's small compared to other monsters. Hell, it's small compared to me. I'd tower over it by several inches. But its size is a form of camouflage. I don't have to look at the open book to know what the notes say about this one. For weeks, I've been studying it, and I've seen it in action. I know that its beautifully muscled body draws other predators in, making them think it is easy prey. But oh no. That delicate-looking monster standing out there is just as deadly as the others ... maybe more so—with those cat-like gold eyes, and soft sweep of midnight hair. It only ever wears a leather kilt, putting its shimmering skin on display along with its lean, toned body. This monster is beauty and strength, created to entice its victims to it.

I watch it as it stares at the back of my house.

Time slips by, minutes then hours. I know I can't wait too long if I'm going to do this, but if I make my move closer to when The Divide is about to go back up, maybe the monster will be distracted by the pull of the magic forcing it back to its realm. It's worked in the past. My squad and I once killed a monster that was snarling and clinging to a dead man. It kept muttering, "No. I'm not done yet. I need more." Its claws sunk into the stomach of the human it was holding as a frustrated growl ripped from its blood-coated lips. It was so concerned with trying to fight the pull of The Divide, it didn't hear the four of us creep up behind it. Its head hit the ground a second before its body disappeared back to the monster realm.

I smile as I focus on the monster outside my house. I settle in. Watching, waiting.

I crack my knuckles as I ask myself the questions I ask every night. What is it doing? Why does it keep showing up? And why ...

I feel like it's protecting me. No, I *know* it's protecting me. But why? My blood-carvings are secure. I'm safe in my house. But ever since Christmas, any time a monster approaches, my starlight monster is there. I've seen it take out and consume monsters three times its size with barely any effort. One look in its eyes ... I'm not sure if it paralyzes or hypnotizes or what, but when it makes eye contact with its victims, they just freeze.

Once, a pack of three monsters stalked down the street, their red, muscled bodies oddly hunched, their spiky arms ending in long, bony, claw tipped fingers. They hissed and snapped their jaws, sniffing the air. They crossed the imaginary line my monster had set up in its head, and it stepped into the light. All three monsters paused, dropping their gazes, then backed away and hurried off. It was impressive. It was ... sexy.

I shake my head. It doesn't matter why that thing is out there. It's a *monster.* Sure, it has been satisfying to watch it chase off, maim, or kill other monsters for the past few weeks, but this increasing pull I feel towards it ... I hate it.

As time ticks by, the monster's gold eyes stay trained on my house, and my gaze stays on it. It's like we're locked together. It's unnerving. I don't like how I'm drawn to look out the window each night to see if it's there, and I despise the relief I feel when it appears. I try not to admit that over the past weeks, I've slept better knowing it's out there. And I *hate* myself for having these feelings.

The monster shifts, drawing me out of my thoughts. My mouth parts slightly, and I lean forward. Whatever light there is to be found in that dark street, it highlights the perfection of the monster. Fuck, it's beautiful. Even knowing it will show up, having seen it out there night after night, every single time I'm entranced. I can't help but wonder what all that shimmery skin feels like. I'm sure its just looking at my house, but it feels like it's staring right at me, and I stare back. I swallow the mix of fear and anticipation as I continue to let my gaze travel over the beautifully deadly monster outside my house. I'm hidden in shadow here in my dark kitchen, and I'm ninety percent sure the monster can't see me. Okay, maybe eight-five percent sure.

My hands tighten on my thighs. I can't do this anymore. This monster has consumed my life. I watch it at night. I wait for it. I think about it all the time. No more!

Fuck it.

Slowly, I stand, letting my right arm hang at my side, gun in hand, the heavy weight resting against my thigh. Moving toe-heel, I back up. Briefly, I consider going out the front to circle my house, but that would expose me to the larger open space of the main street. I'd just be asking for trouble ... or death.

And would that be so bad?

Reece's voice growls through my mind. "*Yes, Max. That would be bad.*"

I'm used to having imaginary conversations with him in my head, so I answer, *I know, babe. Sorry.*

As I slide the side window open, I can't help but stare at the carvings along the sill, the markings stained a dark brown. I wonder if Reece's blood is still there, or has it faded under the layers of all the fresh blood I've added over the years.

I blink away the tears. This is no time for sentimentality.

My old mantra whispers through my head, the words I haven't thought about in a long while. *You are fast, silent, deadly. This is* our *realm. Make the monsters fucking pay.*

I am larger than the monster outside, and though I know my size and strength mean shit against it, I bow up. Flexing my impressive muscles, I grin as I close my eyes and listen. When silence greets me, I lean out, scanning the narrow side street. Other than the overflowing garbage cans, it's clear. Good, the trash may help hide my scent. I lift my leg up and through the window, ducking to silently slip outside.

Time to add another x to my arm. Time to kill the fucking monster that's been stalking me for weeks.

CHAPTER 3

VEX

Every turn—or day as the humans call it—that passes, I tell myself I won't cross to the human realm. And every turn, when The Divide falls, I end up here.

I stare at the back of the townhouse as if I look hard enough, I'll be able to see the male who lives within its walls. My fingers run through my black hair that's bordering on getting too long since it keeps falling in front of my eyes. Movement inside the house catches my attention. My heart rate picks up, and I press further into the shadows. It was just a slight shifting of darkness. I can't be sure I even saw it, or if I'm so eager for a glimpse of him, I'm now imagining him standing in his dark kitchen staring back at me.

I blink. Nothing moves. Releasing my held breath, I comb my fingers through my hair again. I should go back to my realm, to my own house ... away from this human.

But I can't. I'm drawn here. To him. The large male

with the blond hair and the impressive build. The man who moves silently despite his size. The male with sadness in his blue eyes. Since the human Christmas holiday, I've been coming here with an absolute craving to see him, even just glimpses. I thought my obsession would wear off, but ever since I first scented him, it's like I'm being pulled to him. I can't resist.

For hours, I stand as if transfixed, gazing at the house. It's all I *can* do, though every fiber in my being screams to get closer, to get to him somehow.

But I can't. And of course, he never leaves the safety of his home while The Divide is down—though I really wish he would. But humans know better. Well, most of them do. Monsters wouldn't bother coming to this realm if there wasn't fun to be had and power to be gained from consuming human souls.

The low hum of electricity makes my head ache, and I resist the urge to drive my fingers through my hair yet again. In our realm, we don't use electricity. We use magic. We use magic for everything. Power is our currency. We fight to keep what we have. We kill to steal what others possess. The strong survive and thrive. The weak ... don't.

A scraping sound snaps me from my thoughts. My body prickles with awareness. My skin turns from a shimmering blueish-purple of a midnight sky to an oil slick color as I call my magic, activating my hallucinogenic secretions. A feathered grae slinks around the corner at the far end of this row of houses. As I expand my magic, tears well with the discomfort of my power pooling in my eyes, and I know they're glowing in preparation to protect ... *him*. My male is safe in his house behind his blood-carvings, but that doesn't seem to matter as my protective instincts claw at my chest. My entire body screams with the need to keep all threats away from him.

I don't care that he's human. I don't care that *we* are impossible. My body craves him. My thoughts are consumed by him. He is ...

He's *mine.*

The grae's talons click on the asphalt, its bird-like head bobbing. The feathers covering its body sit flush. Its beady eyes lock on me, but it quickly ducks its head to avoid my gaze. There's no blood on the grae's claws or feathers, so it has not satisfied its hunt for more power tonight. I glance at the house on the end of the row, the windows dark, my male somewhere inside.

Stepping into the light of the narrow street, I stare the grae down. *Just one look. Come on. Meet my eyes. Meet your death.*

This grae is smart enough to avoid my eyes, but it won't be able to avoid my touch. It's three times my size, but I'm an anza. We are fast, faster than most. The grae flutters its wings. A squawk comes from its razor-sharp beak that is meant to intimidate. And if this were another place, another time, I would have retreated, not really in the mood for a confrontation. I just want to be left in peace, close to the male who both stirs my blood and calms my soul. But the grae is getting closer, and I won't allow another monster near what is mine.

The heat of my magic deepens, and with an instinctual flex of my lean muscles, I charge. The grae's shriek bounces off the walls of the buildings as it takes off into the air. But I'm faster. It's still looking at the spot where I was standing when I slide underneath its slowly rising body. With an easy leap, I grab one of its thin, bird-like legs. It tries to scratch me with its free leg, but I swing away as my hallucinogenic excretions sink into its skin.

We're now level with the roofs of the townhouses, and I hold on, waiting.

Bending over, the grae aims its deadly beak at my face, but the beating of its wings slows, and we start to fall. The street rushes to meet us, and I let go, landing softly on my bare feet, rolling out of the way. The feathered monster lands hard, the snap of bones telling me it broke at least one leg. But it doesn't react. The grae has fallen into my magic. Its dark eyes stare blankly, its beak open slightly with its panting breaths.

As I approach it, I pat the dirt from my leather kilt. I enjoy the feel of the smooth material against my skin. Clothes weren't really a big thing for monsters before the fall of The Divide, but over the decades, certain aspects of the human realm have rubbed off on us, like clothes. Also, before the fall, most of us looked at gems and metals like a human would look at a flower. Pretty, but of no real use. But now, it's fairly common to see monsters wearing jewelry.

I don't wear bobbles or trinkets, no matter how shiny and tempting they are. I also resisted wearing clothes for years, preferring to leave my skin ... one of my strongest defenses ... bare. But several years ago, this kilt caught my attention when I went to rip it from the human I was eating. The leather felt nice, and the idea of protecting my cock and balls while still being unrestricted was enticing. I don't remember much about the human I took this garment from except that they were small and shapely, so probably a female. They tasted like fear and regret—tart with a depth of flavor like earthy oak. And their soul was delicious, fueling my power, increasing my magic. I recall feeling high from that kill for almost a full turn.

I lick my lips as I look down at the twitching grae. This one won't be as satisfying, but still, I won't waste the magic. I grip one of its wings, my fingers sinking beneath the thick plumage until I hit flesh. More of my secretions sink into its body, and it goes limp. I don't know if it's having a bad hallucination or not, but I don't care.

I rip feathers from flesh, and when one wing is completely bare, I use my magic to lengthen my nails into claws. It takes very little pressure to slice through the grae's skin. A wet tearing sound echoes down the street as I pull a strip of flesh from the monster's body. It blinks as I chew and swallow, the taste light, like, well, as the humans always say, like chicken.

I've nearly stripped one wing clean, when the grae twitches. I sigh, knowing it's unable to move even though it feels the torment of having its skin peeled away by my claws. Looking over its large body, I lose my appetite. This monster's magic is weak and is doing little to boost my power. My fingers dig into the thick feathers around its neck, and with a lightning-quick move, I drive my fangs into its throat. I drink a few swallows before sitting back on my heels. As the grae bleeds out, I look down the street. It's currently empty, but if I leave the body here, it will draw other monsters.

My blond male comes to mind, and I shift to grab the grae's skinny legs. With an easy flex of my muscles, I lean back, ready to carry it from this narrow street to the little park area a few blocks away.

Something hard presses to the back of my head, and I freeze as a deep voice says, "Why have you been watching me?"

It's *him*. He's here. My cock twitches with his nearness, but then fear grips me. He's outside! Outside of his protective barriers.

Fuck.

I turn, moving so fast I know the movement is invisible to the male. A deafening bang rings through my ears, but I easily dodge the bullet screaming towards my face. My magic quickly heals my ringing ears, and before he can pull the trigger again, I hold up my hands in surrender, hoping my small size makes me look like less of a threat. His muscles pull taut, and there's not even the slightest tremble in his arm as he holds the gun pointed at my forehead. I'm fast enough to avoid the bullets, even this close, but I'd prefer it if he didn't open fire on me.

Up close, he is ... perfection. His short sleeve shirt hugs his torso, and I know from my weeks of stalking him that those pants stretch over a firm, round ass. I swallow the sudden flood of saliva, resisting the urge to ... lick him. Keeping my voice soft, I say, "You shouldn't be—"

His presence is a distraction, because before I know it, his large hand wraps around my throat, cutting off my air. Shit, he's *touching* me. And while my body immediately craves more, I'm too panicked to really appreciate it. I try to pull back the magic creating my secretions. My skin loses its oil-slick coating and returns to my natural midnight color.

The male shakes me, his voice rumbling in what I assume is anger, but the tone has my cock hardening even more as he says, "Why have you been watchi ..."

His words trail off as his eyes glaze over. Shit, I wasn't fast enough. His hand falls from my neck, and I cough, dragging in deep breaths. I miss his touch, even though it was rough and painful. Shit. I'm in deep trouble with this male.

He starts to sway, and I lunge forward, wrapping my arms around his broad chest. Easing him to the ground, I cradle his head in my lap. My gaze lands on the gun where it fell to the street. I scowl at it, having felt the sting of a bullet before. While I easily healed the wound, I'm not eager to repeat the experience.

But because I know it will make him feel better once he wakes up, I reach over, pick up the gun and slide it into one of the large pockets along his outer thigh.

Staring down at him, my gaze traces his sharp cheeks, the way his blond hair falls over his forehead, his pink lips held slightly open with his breaths. Is his hair as soft as it looks?

His fingers clench, and I know whatever hallucinations my magic has sent him into are bad. I ... I want to ease his discomfort. I *need* to. I rest my fingers on his face. His skin is warm and smooth. I crave to feel more of him, but as I watch, his cheeks flushed, and sweat beads on his forehead. His breaths are coming too fast. He moans, then his back arches off the ground as his teeth clench. His tight shirt is darkening with sweat, and a scream rips from his throat.

Fuck. I've seen this before. He didn't absorb that much of my drug, but his mind has gone to a dark place. His body is shutting down. He's dying.

No!

My healing ability eats away at my magic, the burn almost painful as I shove my power into the human in my lap. It's slow work. Too slow. It's easy for me to heal damage, physical or mental, from another monster or human. But right now, it's like I'm fighting myself. I'm asking my magic to cleanse my magic from this human. It's resisting, and it hurts.

The Divide begins to scrape at me, its icy pull a painful contrast to my scorching power. Fuck. If I'm pulled away now, my human will die. I've got to do something. But what?

Splaying my hands on either side of his face, I lean

over as I tilt his head back, forcing his glazed gaze to meet mine. I push my magic into my eyes until I see the reflection of their glow on his face. With the hypnosis in place, I command, "Open and drink."

His lips part on a sob of pain that tears at my heart. Wherever he is in his mind must be terrible. I release him and rip into my wrist with my teeth. Holding my arm above his lips, I clench and unclench my fist to let my blood flow into his mouth. I have no idea if this will work, but I have to try.

I'm tense, my back aching as I brace for some conscious part of his mind to revolt at the taste of my blood, but he calms slightly and licks his lips, nearly drawing a groan from my mouth. My cock stiffens, rubbing against the back of his head through the thick leather of my kilt. He swallows faster, as if eager for my taste.

Fuck, he's gorgeous. As if in a trance myself, I lower my wrist to his mouth. I release my groan; the sound rumbling from my chest as he seals his lips to my skin and sucks. Hard. Every pulse of my blood echoes through my cock. Every time his tongue brushes my skin, my balls draw up. It's like he's sucking my soul out through my wrist.

I gaze down at my male in wonder. I already know a lot about him, but I want to know more.

The week after Christmas, I came across a xani hunched over the lifeless body of a human. I watched as the monster shredded the human's clothes and tossed them aside before tearing into its meal. It was so engrossed in its task, it didn't see me as I snuck to the discarded clothes. Luckily, I found what I was looking for, a phone. I pocketed the small device, and I've used it extensively over the past few weeks. Even after the service shut off, I figured out how to push my magic into it to access the internet and keep it powered up.

I've done my research on my male, so I know already, but I have to hear it ... from his lips.

Looking back down into his hazy blue eyes, I see the reflection of my own eyes flaring a bright gold. My hypnosis magic takes hold once again, and I pull my arm away from his mouth as I whisper, "Give me your name."

He reaches for my wrist, grabbing my arm as he says, "Max."

Max indeed. Kind of on the nose, but I like it. It suits him. He pulls my wrist back to his lips and begins drinking again. *Fuuuuuck.* His eyes are still glazed, and I know he doesn't realize what he's doing. With every greedy suck of his mouth against my skin, pleasure builds, and I realize I'm about to come. By sheer willpower, I keep myself under control, but I can't pull away.

He's mine and he can have all of me if that's what he wants.

The Divide wraps around me and pulls. Shit. Keeping my wrist pressed to my male's mouth, I curl myself over his body, holding him. I hope beyond hope that the magic in my blood will trick The Divide into thinking this man is a monster and pull him through with me. Then I can finish healing him. Then I can ...

CHAPTER 4

MAX

Why am I here? No. Please no. The street posts drop pools of light onto the pavement, illuminating the scene before me. I'm sweating, my perspiration mixing with the blood of the two monsters lying dead at my feet. I'd feel satisfaction at those deaths if it weren't for my friend's bodies sprawled on the street ahead. Javid's arm is gone, his eyes staring blankly at the summer night sky. Will's gut is ripped open, his intestines spilling out, sheer agony etched on his lifeless face. I can't help but be thankful Trevor, Julie, and Adam didn't come on this hunt.

Now's not the time to mourn. Not yet. Checking my gun, I count four rounds. I yank my hunting knife out of the skull of the bulbous monster at my feet. Wiping the blood off on my pants, I slide the blade into its sheath. My other pistol is still holstered, and my rifle is slung over my back.

A gurgle draws my attention a few yards down the

street. Reece is kneeling over a monster he's been fighting, and with a sure, confident movement, he stabs it in the chest. The monster gurgles again, some wet substance coming from its grotesque mouth as Reece literally rips its heart out. Tossing the large organ on the ground, Reece stands, wiping his hands on his pants. His gaze finds me, and he smiles, looking around. That smile falters when he spots Javid and Will. Running his still slightly bloody hands through his hair, he swears before looking back at me.

"You okay?"

I nod. "You?"

He starts to stride towards me, his eyes devouring me. "Yeah. Fuck, Max. There were more here than the report said. We should have brought more of the team."

Dread steals my words. Something isn't right. Something bad is coming. I look around, but there's nothing. The only sounds are Reece's light footsteps and the rumble of our running SUV behind me.

As if in slow motion, I focus on Reece. His mouth is moving, but I can't hear him. I want to sprint to him, to shout a warning, to do ... something. But I'm stuck in this nightmare, unable to change what is coming.

Behind Reece, a piece of the shadows peels away like black smoke. It hangs in the air for a second, and then it moves. At least I think it moves. Maybe it teleports. Whatever it does, it's so fast, I can't track it. In a blink, Reece disappears into the darkness. His hand punches out of the shadows like he's reaching through black curtains. His fingers strain towards me, his scream driving into my heart.

Too late, I find the ability to move. I run as the shadows solidify into a beast with patchy fur, claws, rows of teeth, and yellow eyes. I swear it grins at me before snapping its jaws around my boyfriend's shoulder and neck.

Reece's gaze lands on me, and through the agony he mouths, "I'm sorry. I love you."

The monster tears Reece apart, and even when my love's eyes glaze over, the screaming continues. It's me. Closing the distance, I fire off the remaining rounds in my pistol before switching to my other one. Round after round spears through smoke and shadow. I draw my knife, slashing at anything that looks solid. Claws sharper than my blade slice my side, my leg, my shoulder. The monster is toying with me. But if I'm going down, this fucker is going with me. In the chaos, I force myself to center my breathing. As I slash and stab and shoot, I wait. I watch.

I find my chance, slamming my eight-inch knife into the monster's eye. It shrieks, its putrid breath blowing across my face as I scream my rage and sorrow. I twist the blade, but ... the monster goes still, its good eye tracking me.

No. This isn't how it happened. It died. I cut it apart until there was nothing but flesh and blood and bone. Then I burned it.

The nightmare shifts, and Reece's voice comes out of the shadow monster's mouth. "Your fault."

I stumble back, leaving the knife buried in the monster's eye, but it just grins at me. "Your fault, Max. Why didn't you save me?"

No. No. No.

The monster laughs with Reece's voice, and I fall to my knees, covering my ears. The monster grabs my hair, its claws digging into my scalp. Blood drips down my face, turning the world red as the monster shakes me. Reece's voice comes out strong and accusing. "Your fault, Max. Your fault. Your fault. Your fault."

. . .

My body jerks as I'm ripped from the ... nightmare? Hallucination? I manage to keep the gasp of despair from escaping my lips, but it's there in my throat, making it hard to breathe. It's dark beyond my closed eyelids, and that doesn't help. I don't know where I am, and I can tell by the feel and scent—something sweet, like chocolate—that this isn't my bed. Why am I alive? I guess it doesn't matter. That's the monster's mistake.

Staying still, I slowly crack my eyes open. A stark white plaster ceiling stares back down at me. Large worn wood beams add texture and warmth. From the corner of my eye, I get a glimpse of a wide window, confirming it is still dark out. This room must be on a higher floor because there are no buildings or trees visible. Heavy drapes that look like velvet pool on the floor on either side of the glass. Behind the thick velvet, sheer white curtains soften the look. I imagine they would drift and dance prettily in a breeze.

Fuck, Max. Pay attention. You were attacked by a monster ... a monster who has been stalking you. And now you're in a strange bed. Why are you admiring the drapes? Idiot.

I blink back up at the high ceiling. Wiggling my toes, I feel my boots. Good. I flex my thighs, feeling my pants, and surprisingly, the weight of my gun in my side pocket. Either the monster was extremely stupid or exceptionally confident. My empty holster is still secure inside my waistband. Everything is accounted for. But where am I?

My fingers slowly curl into the soft bedding, sending more of that sweet scent to my nose. I sit up with a groan. The dark room swirls, and nausea floods my mouth with saliva. I run my hand down my face, managing to keep myself from throwing up. Besides the slight tremor in my hands, I seem to be okay.

Shadows hide a lot of the room, reminding me of the shadow monster that killed Reece. I HATE the dark, but I don't let that weakness rule me ... or at least I try not to let it send me into a panic attack.

I need to figure out where I am. Has The Divide gone back up?

Shuffling to the window, my breath fogs the glass. It wasn't that cold tonight. I can't see much, but I am indeed on what looks like the second floor of wherever I am. I could jump ...

Turning, I observe what I can see of the dark room. Light wood tables stand on either side of the large bed. Gold filigree decorates the edges and each of the handles. They are feminine, but the solid build also gives a masculine edge to the furniture. Thick rugs overlap and cover nearly the entire stone floor. A large plaster fireplace, sitting cold and unlit, adorns the far wall, holding more menacing shadows. A velvet sofa sits in front of the fireplace, and to the right, an open door reveals the edge of a glass shower—a bathroom, so probably not an exit.

I head towards another door. Wrapping my hand around the knob, I stand still and listen. Nothing. I squeeze the handle tighter as I open the door, as if my grip will keep the hinges from squeaking. But there's no noise, and when I peek in ... a library? The smell of leather and paper wafts from the room, and curiosity itches at my fingers to go explore, but I don't see another way out in this room, so I turn, striding towards the final door.

I'm only two steps away when a flash of bluish-purple color moves from my left. It's awkward getting my pistol out of my pocket, but I wrap my hand around the grip, holding the weapon before me with a hand that only trembles slightly. Little win.

A monster ... my monster ... stands between me and the door.

Fuck. That means the Divide is still down. But wait, we're inside ... someone's house. What about the blood-carvings? What the hell is going on?

But damn. It's beautiful. Desire stirs, and I angrily shut it down. I've been watching it for weeks. I know the perfection of its form is just another weapon this monster uses to catch its prey. But being in this enclosed space, being so close to it ... I wouldn't mind falling victim to its charms. Its shimmering skin hugs lean muscles. It has the toned body of a runner. That damned leather kilt swishes as it shifts, its golden cat-like eyes watching me. For one sinful moment, I wonder what my starlight monster is hiding under that singular piece of clothing. I grit my teeth against the unwelcome thought. I have to be cautious here. Surely, The Divide will go back up soon. Any minute now.

My monster runs its hand through its black hair, its abs flexing as if every single move it makes is meant to seduce. And it's working. Before I know what I'm doing, I take a step towards it. Fuck. I grit my teeth, forcing myself to remain where I am. *Not another step, Max. I don't care how badly you want to. It's a monster. Are you going to let a pretty face and beautiful body with a sexy protective streak erase the memory of what they did to Reece?*

My monster blinks, dropping its arm with a sigh and opens its mouth to speak.

I don't think. I react. My ears ring, and the sharp scent of gunpowder fills my nose as I fire three times. My monster simply disappears and reappears a step away, and the bullets tear through the door. The spent casings thud onto the soft rug under my feet, and I blink in astonishment.

Okay.

Suspecting it was the skin to skin contact with this thing that sent me into that nightmare of a hallucination, I kick, aiming for its knee. Again, it simply steps out of range as if I'm moving in slow motion. Well, I guess to it, I am moving sluggishly with my paltry human speed. The ringing in my ears seems to echo and bounce around my skull as I fire again. And again. Over and over. Each time, I try to anticipate where the monster will move to dodge, but its blurred form easily dances out of the way of each bullet.

My finger tenses on the trigger again, but I realize the slide is locked back. It's empty, and I don't have a fresh mag on me. I take a step back, keeping my eyes on the monster. My ears are still ringing, and I fight the urge to stick my finger in one and give it a wiggle.

My monster is not even breathing hard, its muscled chest rising and falling steadily. It holds up its hands. "You can relax, Max. You are safe here."

With the ringing still in my ears, it sounds like its words are being funneled through water, but its voice is somehow both soft and strong. Comforting. But wait, it knows my name? Fuck. I take another step back, and when it doesn't move, I take another, and another, moving faster. I'll jump out the goddamned window if I must.

There's no point in holding my empty gun, so I slide it into my holster. Whatever my monster did to me seems to be lingering. The edges of my vision start to tunnel, but I shake it off. I *will not* pass out now.

My monster finally moves to follow me as it says, "Take it slow, Max. The drug is out of your system, but you might still be weak."

The ringing in my ears has finally faded, making its

voice clear, soothing, enticing. The way it says my name ... it's almost intimate.

The heel of my boot hits a wall, and I reach back feeling the cold glass of the window. In a blink, my monster is right before me, grabbing my wrist. "Don't. You can't go out there, Max. It's not safe. Just, please, let me explain."

I yank back, and it lets me go. Panic starts to rise, and my heart races. My eyes dart towards the door, but I know I can't beat my monster there. I rub my wrist where it grabbed me, my brows scrunching in concern. How much time do I have before I start falling into the hallucinations again?

The monster glances at my hand, then shakes its head. "My touch is only harmful when my secretions are active. I control it with my magic, though sometimes it just happens if I'm in danger, like a defensive reflex. But right now"—it holds up its hand—"see, my skin is dry. You're safe."

I stare at the monster's skin, waiting for the dizziness, or for the walls to start swirling or something. When nothing happens, breathe a little easier as I ask, "So, you secrete ... what? Drugs?" It nods with a shrug. I don't know why my monster is in a sharing mood, but every piece of information is another weapon I can use against it. I ask, "And your eyes?"

It looks up at me. "Only when they glow. I can ... hypnotize."

"So, you drug your prey and control their minds."

Again, it nods, holding up its delicate hands. "I can also sharpen my nails into claws, but they aren't as strong as some others. I have fangs, but I don't have wings, or a barbed tail. I don't spit poison or have a shriek that bursts eardrums. I can't shoot bone shards from my hands or shift into a beast form. My body as you see it is all I have."

I can't help but look at all the exposed twilight skin. It is beautiful. And I have to stop thinking like that. I sneer. "You seem to be doing alright."

The glimmering skin around its cheeks darkens. Is it blushing? It runs its hands through its hair again. "Don't misunderstand. My kind are deadly. Even though we are small compared to other monsters"—its gaze travels down my body and back up, and I almost shiver at the look in its eyes—"and even some humans, but we *are* predators. We are evolved beings; our bodies honed to protect us and deliver death."

"What are you?"

"I am an anza." It presses its hand to its chest. "My name is Vex."

It's on the tip of my tongue to ask how it knows my name, but it doesn't matter. Instead, I ask, "Where am I?

No answer. I stare into its gold eyes, and it stares back.

Okay.

I take a step to my left, and it copies me. I circle the bed, my monster following. My voice drops into the commanding tone I used back in my hunter days when I led our team into the streets to fight the monsters. It's a voice that demands answers. "Vex, where am I?"

Its eyes widen, and its lips fall open. "You ... gods, I spent so many nights imagining what it would sound like for you to say my name, but hearing it just now ..."

What the actual fuck? There's a shimmer in its eyes. Is it ... about to cry?

A pang of ... something stutters in my heart. I ignore it. I've trained myself well over the years to hide from my feelings. I keep quiet. Another long silence fills the room, but I wait. Waiting is good. Every second that ticks by is another bringing us closer to The Divide going back up, then this fucker will poof out, and I can get out of wherever it is I am. I can go home, regroup, and come up with a plan to take this monster out once and for all.

That's what I want. *It is.*

Reece's voice laughs through my mind. "*You trying to convince yourself?*"

Shut up.

I find myself once again letting my gaze wander. My monster's toned muscles rippling with each subtle movement. Its black hair keeps falling over its gold eyes, and I bite the inside of my cheek as it pushes the strands back. Why do I keep getting distracted by this monster?

Reece sighs. "*Because you're drawn to it, and that's oka—*"

I shut down that train of thought and angrily answer back. *No! I'm simply reacting to the defenses of my monst ... of* the *monster. Nature designed it to draw in, to seduce, to lure. That's it. That's all I'm feeling.*

The Reece in my head doesn't respond.

I'm pulled away from my thoughts when, finally, the monster speaks. "First, let me say that ... you were dying. The hallucinations were ... they were bad. I had no choice." I crack my middle finger knuckle with my thumb, uneasy as it says, "You are in my house. This is my room."

I just blink at it.

It sighs again, shifting on the balls of its feet as if it's going to take another step towards me, but then it rocks back. It even has pretty feet.

No. Stop it. Stop looking.

It stays where it is, saying, "Like I said, you were dying." It holds up its hands, palms up. "I have healing ability, but it was my magic that was killing you, and I found it quite difficult to cancel out my own magic. I ... I didn't have time. The Divide was pulling at me. You would have died."

Tension coils up my spine with every word. It can't possibly mean ...

It drops its head. "You are in my realm, Max."

Panic threatens to steal my breath. I'm in the monster's realm? "How?"

"I ... I used the hypnotic power of my eyes to compel you ... I um, well." His eyes lift to meet mine. "You drank my blood, and The Divide thought you were a monster, so it pulled you through with me." Its words speed up, but a deadly calm spreads through me as it goes on. "I didn't know what else to do. You were dying, Max. Had I left you on the street, you would have ... I was able to heal you once I got you back here. You might still feel a little unsteady, but you are fine now. You are safe here, Max. I promise."

I barely hear the last words as I lunge to my right. My hand wraps around the glass of water sitting on the bedside table. In one swift movement, I smash the glass against the table and rip the broken end across my wrist. I don't care if I die, I can't live with monster blood flowing through my veins.

I won't.

The monster is before me before I can blink. It's so fast, I didn't see it move. It shouts, "Max! No!"

It tries to grab my bleeding arm, but I yank away, blood splashing against the wall. I swing at the monster with my other fist, but it easily dodges my punch. Backing up a step, my legs hit the bed, and I watch as my hot blood gushes down my arm, dripping onto the rug. I clench my fist, willing the blood to spill faster. The dark pool spreads through the lush weave of the carpet. I smile. I hope it was terribly expensive, because now it's ruined. *It's the little wins, you know?* Reece used to say that.

Using my other hand, I squeeze the tear in my flesh, feeling slightly dizzy as my blood pours out. Almost in a panic, I grip my wrist tighter. Faster. The blood needs to come out faster.

Fingers press to my wrist, gentle ... trembling? "That's enough, Max."

I try to pull away, but even though its grip is light, it's as if my arm is locked in a vice. I try once more to free myself of its warm touch, but then I'm distracted by a tingling around my wrist. Glancing down, I watch, amazed as the deep gash in my arm stops bleeding then knits together. In a matter of seconds, there's nothing but a faint white line. And then even that is gone.

Lifting my gaze from my wrist, I look at the monster in front of me. The room fades away as it smiles. Fuck me. I hate myself right now because damn if I don't want my monster to keep smiling at me like that. It's so beautiful. Like midnight come to life.

Damn it.

Its fingers lightly wrap around my wrist. It looks at me, its cat-like eyes traveling over my face with ... reverence? Some of its black hair has fallen over its eyes again, and I have the obscene urge to comb it back with my fingers.

Fuck, Max. Get it together. It's a monster.

"A very pretty monster that is being kind to you right now."

But it's this monster's fault I'm here in the first place.

"It saved you. Stop being an ass."

My monster shifts again, and I can't help but look at its eyes. There's almost a pleading look to them as it says,

"Please, don't hurt yourself, Max. I will make sure you get home safely once The Divide goes back down."

I glance back at my wrist, wondering if I bled enough. Will The Divide continue to pull me back here, to the realm of monsters? If so, I'll have to bleed myself a little every few hours until I'm purged of this blight.

I realize my monster still has a hold of my wrist, and I slide from its grip. It lets me. I'm under no illusion that it couldn't easily overpower me with its magic or deceptive strength.

Reclaiming my own power, I meet its gaze head on, hoping I look steadier than I feel. "Why did you bother saving me? Why have you been watching me?"

CHAPTER

VEX

Why have I been watching Max. That's a loaded question, and the answer will definitely freak him out. Honestly, I'm amazed he didn't wake up and immediately start shooting at me. I mean, the shooting did happen, but not right away.

It's the little wins.

I move to run my hand through my hair but stop myself. I'm sure it's already sticking out all over the place. And now I want to run my hands through my hair to fix it. Ugh.

Taking a slow breath, I start to lift my head, but I can't seem to make eye contact while I say, "I saved you, and I've been … watching you for the same reason … and it's complicated."

I'm a coward. I know it. But I'm a monster, and he's a human. And not just any human.

All monsters know about the bands of humans that

take to the streets during the hours when we come to their realm. Honestly, most monsters like the tenacious hunters. Sometimes, they are the only humans available to hunt. It really is quite fun to run down prey that thinks it's a predator.

Max used to be one of those hunters.

Max has a very limited presence online, but there were some things about him to be found. Like the picture I saved to the little phone that's now sitting in my bedside table. It's an old photo, the date from twelve years ago. Max is smiling, his face painfully sexy. His arm is slung over the shoulders of another man who is laughing. A large armored vehicle stands behind the two men, and the caption reads, '*Reece and Max. Two members of our local hunter squad. Heroes fighting back.*'

Dread and jealousy weighed me down when I first saw that photo. I searched and searched but couldn't find much else on the handsome Reece. All I know is that he doesn't live with Max, and I have a sinking suspicion I know what happened to him. Hunters aren't known to live long lives.

I have heard Max speak on his phone to someone called Peter, but his voice was never very happy when he talked to him, so I don't know what their relationship is.

Max cracks his knuckles with his thumb, a scowl on his face. "Complicated? I'm a smart guy. I think I'll be able to follow."

It's there on the tip of my tongue, as if the words themselves are eager for him to hear them. But I swallow them down, and when I remain silent, he ... growls. I didn't know humans did that. I like it. And so does my cock. It twitches against the leather of my kilt, and I shift my weight, hoping Max won't notice.

Crossing his large arms, he glares at me, and even

though there's menace in his eyes, I can't help but wonder what it would feel like to have that look aimed at me in a commanding way.

Fuck. I want it. I want him.

He's so close. I've touched him. His skin is soft, but even the slightest pressure brought my fingers against hard muscle. And his scent ... like a crisp breeze blowing off a frozen lake.

I realize I'm staring when Max's gravelly voice breaks the silence once more. "Are you going to keep showing up? Keep watching me for whatever reason?"

I could say no, because there's no need, since I intend to keep him. But I'm not sure *how* to keep this large male at my side, not yet. So, I answer honestly.

"Yes." *Because I physically can't stay away from you.*

Max stares at me, his jaw flexing as he grinds his teeth. There's a little shadow of hair dusting his face, blond as the hair on his head, and I wonder what he'd look like with a beard. And now I'm wondering what that beard would feel like scraping against my inner thighs ...

Maybe it's the blush staining my cheeks, or the heat that is certainly in my eyes, but Max's lips part, and a little puff of air escapes ... almost a gasp. He's searching my face, and the look in his eyes ... Maybe I want him too much, because I swear there's desire there.

Max's gaze hardens. "Fuck this."

I see his movements clearly, knowing what's coming, but for some reason I let him. With surprising speed for a human, he grabs a piece of the broken glass. I should have cleaned that up right away, if only to keep him from harming himself again. But that's not his intent right now.

Max takes the single step that separates us, and despite the violence in his eyes, I savor his nearness. The bite of the glass entering my flesh burns. He slams the jagged piece into my neck, actually hitting my carotid. Good aim. My healing ability immediately focuses on the wound, keeping me from bleeding out, but I don't let it heal completely. Max needs control right now. He needs to feel powerful. So, I give him this.

I reach for the glass shard as Max backs away, his hand stained with my black blood. A sliver of panic enters his eyes, and he looks around, I assume for somewhere to wipe my blood off. I grab the small edge of the glass that is sticking out of my neck, wincing. It's in there pretty deep. Pain spears through my throat as I say, "My blood won't hurt you, Max. I won't hurt you. Not again. I promise."

As I start to work the shard out of my neck, more of my blood spills down my chest. Damn it, I'm going to have to clean my kilt before it stains the leather.

A new expression falls over Max's face, and I can't read it. For a long moment, he stares at my blood, then his tongue flicks over his lips. Is he recalling my taste? Does he want more?

I'm a fool. Of course he doesn't.

A sound between a growl and a scream rips from his lips. He grabs the bedside table, and with an impressive flex of his muscles, heaves the heavy furniture at me.

Fuck, he's strong.

I step to the side to avoid the flying furniture but get distracted as Max sprints for the door. I grunt as the edge of the table clips my shoulder, sending the glass deeper into my skin from where I still have a hold of it.

Damn it all!

The door bangs against the wall, and Max flees into the hallway. I can't let him leave. I can't let him go outside the wards surrounding my house. The monsters ...

No! Max is mine!

In a flash, I rip the slippery glass out of my neck,

healing the deep wound quickly. Using my speed, I dart from my bedroom. He's already thundering down the stairs. With a blur of motion, I speed past him, noticing the growing panic under the fury in his eyes. He's scared. I don't blame him, but still, it hurts.

Coming to a stop at the bottom of the stairs, I hold up my hands. Max's eyes go even wider, surprised at my sudden appearance, but he adapts. Of course he does. He wouldn't have survived long as a hunter without having honed reflexes.

Max grips the railing and leaps over, landing softly on the dark wood floor. He sprints through my living room. I know he doesn't know where he's going, but maybe it's some ingrained intuition that's taking him in the direction that will lead him though my dining hall and into the kitchen ... where there are knives. Lots of knives. And ... a door leading outside to my gardens.

Shit.

I race through my house, reaching the archway that leads into the kitchen just before Max gets there. He skids to a stop, his boots squeaking on the wood floor. He's not breathing that hard, but still, his tight shirt stretches with each of his inhales.

Utter shock freezes me in place as he stalks ... towards me. He stares me down, looming over me as he stops just before his broad chest touches mine. A single brow climbs his forehead, and he ... touches me. Even knowing what I'm capable of doing to him with my magic, he presses his fingers to my neck. He's testing me. I let him. I'll let him do whatever he wants if he'll just keep his fingers pressed to my skin.

His touch is feather light, and right over the place where he stabbed me with the glass. His gaze follows his fingers as they trace the curve of my neck, down to my shoulder. I can't breathe. I feel like I could die right there, and at the same time, fly to the stars. This is ...

Max steps past me. I'm too stunned to stop him. Are my feelings that clear on my face that he used them against me? Smart. I hear the slide of metal over metal, and I turn just as he throws a butcher knife at me. I duck, and the blade sails past, thudding into the wall. Another glint of steel flashes in the light, and I dodge that one as well. Max backs up through the kitchen, throwing knife after knife at me. Why do I have so many fucking knives?

Reaching behind him, Max grabs the door handle. The last blade, a small paring knife, is in his other hand. I've tried gentle submission, but I can't let him leave, so I try another tactic. Raising a brow, I smirk and glance over my shoulder, waving at the knives sticking out of my kitchen wall.

"You can throw that last one, but we both know it would be wasted. If you intend to leave the safety of my home and go out there, you better hold onto that one. You won't last long, but that may give you a few more seconds."

Placing my hands on my hips, I tap my foot on the floor, waiting for him to see reason. *Please let him see reason.*

Max keeps his grip on the door handle, staring at me. His shoulders relax just slightly, and relief begins to pour through me, but then he rips the door open and sprints outside.

FUCK!

CHAPTER 6

MAX

Cold air blasts against my face. The snap of my boots against the flagstone patio quickly turns to the crunch of gravel underfoot. There are no other houses, no other buildings at all within sight. I have to get away. I have to get home. Surely, my monster was lying. As I draw in a lungful of air, I take in the taste and smell of being out in the country. Clean air, plant life, the slight decay of leaves ... Large trees line the path I'm sprinting down, and ... shit ... little orbs of light magically dance in the air, illuminating the way.

Double shit. Maybe Vex wasn't lying. Am I really in the monster realm?

I skid to a stop, debating on if I should keep running or go back. The monster I know is better than the ones out here that I don't, right?

Brighter light to my left distracts me, and I see ... a garden? Neat, raised beds hold colorful vegetables. Larger orbs of what look like sunlight bob and float around the plants.

I swear at myself. "Focus, Max. You can't afford to panic or get distracted, no matter how curious you are. Concentrate." I know if I don't go back, Vex will come after me.

Why does that give me a thrill?

As if my thoughts summoned my monster, I feel the breeze of Vex blurring past me, but then, a howl tears through the night. I know that sound. It's too deep to be a hellhound, and besides, those like to hunt in packs. This was a singular howl. It must be one of the large werewolf-like monsters.

My thumb presses down on the top of my pointer finger, middle, ring, pinky ... cracking each one. I know how to kill this monster. Remove the head or heart. Both is better. Bring it on. I grip the little knife tighter. It's not much, but it'll get the job done. I just wish I hadn't wasted all my ammo trying to hit the unhittable Vex.

Speaking of my beautiful monster ... Vex's hand presses against my shirt over my chest. "Max, stop. Come back inside. My house is warded. You'll be sa—"

"You brought a human to our realm." The werewolf's voice is gravelly as it stalks around a tree, licking its muzzle. "How?"

Fuck, no. If monsters find out they can bring humans here simply by forcing them to ingest monster blood ...

Before I'm able to say or do anything, Vex turns, holding out his arms ... shielding me. Ridiculous monster.

Reece's voice coos in my head. *"Aww. You like it."*

Vex snaps. "Leave, Jarius. You will get neither answers nor flesh this turn or any other."

The werewolf, Jarius, lifts its snout, its nose twitching. "It smells good. That one has a strong soul." Its gaze lands on me, its eyes narrowing. "I see the fight in you, human. Come. Dance with me. It will be a great battle, and when it's over, I will grant you a quick death. The death of a warrior." Its eyes flick to Vex before coming back to me. "*They* will not give you such mercy. They are pretty enough, but once Vex is done playing with you, they will devour you slowly and painfully."

Adrenaline spikes through me, making my skin tingle. I shift my weight to the balls of my feet, ready to fight.

Vex disappears from before me, and in a blink, reappears right next to Jarius. The werewolf jumps nearly a foot in the air in fright, and I fight to hold back a chuckle. I didn't see Vex move either, but at least it's not me this time that's caught by surprise. Oddly, something in me ... relaxes knowing Vex is here. I slide my free hand into my pocket. Cocking my hip to the side, I watch while listening for the sounds of any other monsters approaching.

I expect Vex's skin to change, or their eyes to start glowing, or at least for their nails to lengthen into claws. But no. They simply grab Jarius before the werewolf can move. With what looks like a simple flex of muscle, Vex snaps Jarius' neck. The werewolf flops to the ground, its tongue lolling between its sharp teeth.

Fuck. Vex is *so strong*.

This time, they don't use their super speed. Instead, Vex walks back to me. Is there a slight sway to their steps? The light from the nearby magic orbs highlights every dip of their lean muscles, their gold eyes bright but not glowing.

That werewolf and Vex seemed to know each other, and I assume Jarius referred to Vex as *they* for a reason. I mean, maybe not, but that pronoun fits my starlight monster. Either, or. Neither, or both. They are simply, Vex.

And why am I worrying over pronouns right now?

"Because a piece of yourself you refuse to acknowledge ... cares."

I shake off Reece's voice as Vex keeps approaching. Their kilt swishes, their toned legs closing the space between us. And those feet ... toes now dusty, but seemingly unbothered by the fine gravel underfoot. Does the cold not bother them?

Vex's voice comes out with a low, almost purr-like sound. "Max, you have to stop looking at me like that."

I grit my teeth, swallowing. I know that. I'm trying to stop, but my body won't listen. Why? Why *them*? Why is it a monster to be the first to stir such strong emotions in me after Reece? I HATE this.

They keep coming, and it's getting harder to breathe. I tell myself to back away. I don't. Vex stops mere inches in front of me, their eyes *devouring* me. I know all too well the high that clings to you after a fight. I see it in their eyes. Fuck, I didn't even do anything, and I'm a little jittery with adrenaline.

Vex lifts a hand, but before their palm makes contact with my chest, I growl. "Don't."

Vex doesn't even flinch as their warm fingers curl into my shirt, their eyes trailing over my body. That scent—sweet but rich—teases my senses. Vex swallows and moves even closer.

Something in my mind snaps. The years of grieving Reece, the toxic flings after his death, the emptiness, Peter leaving me tonight, another lonely Valentine's Day looming ... My hand snaps out, circling Vex's neck. I squeeze just enough, and their lips part beautifully for me. Leaning down, I use my size to intimidate even knowing my monster could easily kill me in a dozen ways. Their eyes flick between mine. There's such longing there, it breaks me even further.

I yank, and they stumble into me. My lips crash against theirs in an angry kiss. I don't even know if this can be called a kiss. There's nothing tender or sweet about it, but Vex melts under me, surrendering. They take my punishing lips and teeth and tongue. I hate how affected I am by them. I've never felt this way before, not even ...

That thought yanks me back. I shove Vex away from me, and we both stare at each other, our chests rising and falling heavily. I try to ignore the growing hardness in my pants, but then I notice ... yes, Vex's kilt is tented slightly. Why do I want to see it? Why do I want to watch them stroke their cock so I can learn how they like to be touched? Why them? I had Reece. I had love. I don't want to feel this way. I *hate* monsters.

But this one ... Fuck. I can't do this. I ...

Vex must see the conflict on my face, because their demeanor changes—their eyes softening, their posture relaxing. "Will you please come inside now? There are still a few hours before The Divide drops."

My eyes flick to Jarius' body, and Vex tsks. "He's not dead. I'd have to rip his heart out."

I nod. "I know."

A single brow lifts on Vex's expressive face, then they smile. "Ah, yes. Your monster book." I can't keep my eyes from going wide in surprise. I know my monster has been watching me, but for them to know about that ...

Vex goes on, "Anyway, he'll heal in a turn or two, depending on how much magic he had before I snapped his no-good neck. Damn joteunn just don't know when to back off. Don't worry, though. Even if he wakes up earlier, he can't get inside. Like I said, my house is warded."

"Joteunn?"

"That's what he is. I've heard you humans call them werewolves, which I guess is close enough, though joteunn don't have a humanoid form. They always look that ugly."

I can't help the laugh that bubbles from my lips, and Vex smiles back. Tilting my head to look up at the stars—so I don't get lost in that smile—I sigh. "So, this is the monster realm. It's ... not what I thought it would be."

It's pretty. It's familiar. So similar to the human side of The Divide. The air is chilly, and there's a light breeze causing goosebumps to surface across my skin. The stars wink overhead. The trees and bushes swaying with soft sounds. It feels calm, peaceful. Not how I should feel in the dark of night. Night for a human in my part of the world is terror and death. I don't know if I've ever gone outside at night without a lick of at least a little fear.

And then the darkness took on a whole new depth when that shadow monster ... when Reece ...

A thought snaps my gaze back to Vex. "Wait, if The Divide is up, that means it's the middle of the day. Why is it dark here?"

Vex's voice is soft as they say, "Welcome to Ekenys. It's perpetually night here."

"No sun? Ever?"

They shake their head. "If we want sunlight we either create it here with our magic, or we travel through to the parts of the human realm where The Divide goes down during the day."

"That's ... I'd miss the sun." I've barely finished my sentence when the floating orbs over in the garden get brighter, splashing us with magical sunlight. It's even warm. I face Vex, meeting their shy smile. So cute.

Wait. What? No. Stop it.

"Come on. They are cute."

Vex's smile slips, their teeth worrying their bottom lip. "I really am sorry, Max. For bringing you here. I know this is the last place you'd ever want to be. If there was another way, I would have—"

I hold up a hand. There's nowhere for me to flee. I can't get home yet, and Vex ... being around them ...

This entire situation is, well ... vexing.

Vex swallows, something almost vulnerable in their eyes. "Please, will you come back inside?"

Reece's voice floats through my mind. *"Vex has shown you that you're safe with them."*

But what if they—

"Max."

The chiding tone I give myself through Reece's voice makes my shoulders slump in defeat. I nod at Vex, and their eyes light up—not with magic, but with what I can only describe as hope. Something unfurls inside me. I ... I don't want to hurt their feelings. I don't want to be the one to dash that hope.

Vexing indeed.

CHAPTER 7

VEX

I start walking back towards my house, looking over my shoulder to see if Max really will follow. He does, and my heart skips a beat.

That kiss. I've never been so totally consumed by anyone or anything. It was better than the strongest flood of new magic. It was ... life altering.

Once back inside my kitchen, I flick my hand, sending my magic to the orbs floating near the high ceiling. Light fills the room, and I notice Max takes a slow breath. The pinched expression around his eyes softens. Does he not like the dark?

Walking around the kitchen island to give myself a moment, I try to convince my cock to relax. Max leans against a counter, crossing his arms. "It's just you in this giant house?"

I nod, moving towards the obscenely large refrigerator, opening the door. "It is a lot of space, but it still feels, I don't know, cozy to me." I duck my head into the refrigerator, avoiding eye contact with Max, letting the cool air calm my overheated skin. "Let me fix you something to eat. What do you like? I probably have it in here somewhere."

Before he can answer, I set a large head of lettuce on the kitchen island. Going back to the fridge again, I grab vegetable after vegetable. We both stay silent as I set cucumbers, a tomato, a bell pepper, carrots, and radishes on the island. I've dreamed of doing this for him so many times.

Uncrossing his arms, Max grips the edge of the counter. "All that come from your garden out there?"

I nod, trying to keep myself from preening. He notices. I duck back behind the fridge door, grabbing a container of cooked beans. When I turn and close the door, Max is right before me. I blink at him. I didn't hear him move. Well done, mate.

Mate. That kiss made everything crystal clear. My heart beats for him, and always will. How lucky I am to have found him in all the world, in all the realms.

I've suspected since Christmas. The night Paine, the dremar, forced me into the human realm to heal his mate, I scented something on the air that tasted like *mine*. My obsession was born. And here he is.

My. Mate.

Max glances at the gathering of vegetables then looks at me with a smirk. "You have not only been watching. You've been paying attention."

I can feel the skin along my cheeks heating with a blush, and I'm pretty sure Max notices. I cross the room, yanking a knife from the wall. "You mean I've been stalking you."

"Your words." There's a hint of humor in his voice, and it gives me hope.

I grab a large bowl and slide a cutting board from a cabinet. The wood thuds loudly on the marble counter, and I start chopping. As the quick *snick snick* of the knife fills the air, I just let the words out. "I've always grown flowers in my gardens. I love my roses with their tempting beauty and their sharp thorns." I duck my head, letting my hair hide as much of my face as it can as I add, "But I added the vegetables soon after I ..."

From the corner of my eye, I see Max's lips twitch with a smile. "After you started stalking me." I shrug, staring down at the cucumber under my knife. I pause but remain silent, so he asks again, "Why, Vex? Why do you show up every night? Why do I ..."

When he doesn't finish his sentence, I finish it in my head. *Why do I feel drawn to you? Why do I have these feelings?* I get it. I saw the lust mixed with the hatred in his eyes after he kissed me. And while it nearly gutted me to see that hate on Max's face, I can't regret that kiss.

It's the little wins.

I give him the only answer I'm strong enough to give, because the truth will surely chase him away. "I can't tell you, Max."

His presence gets closer, not farther away like I expected. I hear him swallow, and from my peripheral, I see him watching my hands as they maneuver the knife and veggies. Scooping up the pile of diced cucumber, I add it to the nearly overflowing bowl.

Max chuckles, breaking some of the tension, but I nearly swoon on the spot at the deep, rumbling sound. He nods at the salad. "That's enough to feed a family of four."

I lean into his levity, and smile. "Well, Max, you

certainly live up to your name." I sweep a hand at his muscled body. "I mean, look at you."

He chuckles a little louder, and fuck if my cock doesn't start to get hard again. I blurt out, "So, how do you like it?" He raises one brow, and I nearly choke on my tongue. "The salad. Sorry. How do you like your salad dressed?"

With his grin lighting up his face, he says, "Oil and vinegar is fine, if you have it."

I nod, peeling myself away from his gaze. Grabbing the glass bottles off the counter behind me, I pray this isn't another ploy. But if he smashes the bottle and tries to stab me with the shards, so be it. I hand the oil to him, my imagination shifting to him using it for a much ... naughtier purpose. Fuck, I'm not going to be able to hide this erection for much longer.

My voice waivers slightly as I say, "I'll let you do it. I tend to like my salad drowning in dressing."

He takes the bottle. As he upturns it, drizzling the contents over the salad, he looks around my large kitchen. "I'm surprised."

"By what?"

The oil bottle clinks softly as he sets it down before picking up the vinegar. "A lot. But, to start, I'm surprised how nice everything is. This kitchen ..." He looks around, his eyes landing on my eight-burner stove. "I mean, you had a bit of a snack outside my house earlier. I thought all monsters just ate flesh and consumed blood."

I try not to be offended by his remark. Of course my house is nice. I may be a monster, but I still like to live comfortably. Why wouldn't I?

I slide a fork over the marble counter, hoping I'm not handing him another weapon. He picks it up, stabbing into the bowl instead of my flesh as I say, "Yes, we do ...

but most of us only consume others for the magic. I enjoy a good meal of salad or pasta."

Max pauses his chewing. "Shit. I'm sorry. That sounded bad, didn't it. I just meant—"

I hold up a hand. "It's fine, Max. I understand."

He resumes chewing but keeps his blue gaze on me. After he swallows, he asks, "So, eating monsters and … humans gives you power?"

I glance at his salad. "You want to talk about this while eating?"

He stuffs a loaded fork in his mouth, the crunch of his chewing loud as he says, "If I'm stuck here, I might as well learn all I can."

Ah. He wants information. Of course he does. He may not go out on the hunts anymore, but he's still *that* man. A man who won't sit back and just let things happen around him. Fine. If that's what will keep him here with me, I'll tell him whatever he wants to know. I'll sell out any and every monster's secrets for just another moment with Max.

And now I'm picturing Max and me hunting together, taking down monsters. I imagine him standing guard over our kill as I consume its magic, and then we go back to his place or mine, and …

I shake myself out of my thoughts and answer his question. "Yes. Consuming the flesh and blood of other monsters gives us their magic. Power can be bartered or traded, but it's not nearly as potent. We don't really know what it is about humans—so very few of you still have any actual magic left—but some believe it's your souls that feed our magic. Whatever it is, it's … powerful."

Even though it's probably understood, I realize I just admitted to eating humans. I wait for the outrage. Instead,

Max asks around another mouthful of veggies, "Some humans have magic?"

That's what he got caught up on? I almost laugh. "Yes, but it is exceedingly rare. Ages ago, it was more prevalent, but that was way before The Divide fell. Back then, only the strongest of monsters could get through to your realm. And even then, only at certain times ... Samhain, any of the solstices ... there are natural times when The Divide ... thins."

Max nods, and I can see him formulating his next question, but I slip in one of my own. "Can I ask you something?"

"You can ask. We'll see if I answer."

I hold back all the questions about him that press against the back of my lips. Instead, I ask one that I don't think he'll mind answering.

"The human holiday of Valentine's Day is coming soon. Do you ... have a valentine?"

CHAPTER 8

MAX

I pause with the fork halfway to my mouth. Did my monster just ask me if I have a valentine for Valentine's Day? I set the fork in the bowl and place the bowl on the counter. Bracing a hand on the island, I lean a hip against the marble to fully face Vex.

"You know about Valentine's Day?"

They mirror my posture, the pose much more delicate looking on them as they nod. "I've done some research. To be honest, most of your human holidays make absolutely no sense." I chuckle. They're not wrong. "The winter holidays, I kind of get. At least most of them have something to do with the solstice. And celebrating the birth of a god is nothing new."

They reach for the salad bowl, raising a brow. I nod, and Vex picks it up, grabbing the fork I was using and spears a few pieces of lettuce and a bright red tomato. As they bring it to their lips, I swallow, transfixed by the flex of their jaw as they chew.

They continue. "Halloween seems fun. It would be exceedingly delightful if you still did the trick-or-treat thing at night."

I huff. "Yeah, send humans out dressed like monsters, then throw real monsters into the mix. Sounds like a fun time."

Vex shrugs. "For the monsters." They wave the fork. "Anyway, once I went deeper into my research, I realized just how many holidays you humans celebrate. New Years, Christmas, Ramadan, Diwali, Day of the Dead, Hanukkah, Thanksgiving ..."

"Don't forget Divide Remembrance Day."

Vex nods. "Yes. It was quite a day to remember."

"For different reasons by both sides." I crack my knuckle, wondering if it's even worth asking the question burning in my mind, but I go for it. "Why did The Divide fall? Did someone or something tear it down?"

They shake their head. "No one knows. There are rumors, of course, but nothing has been confirmed."

"If it was done by someone, wouldn't that monster be considered a hero in this realm?"

Vex turns, placing the almost empty bowl in the large sink. They grip the edge of the counter, head bowed for a moment before turning back to me. "I guess. But that's assuming it was a monster who did it."

I reel back a step before steadying myself. A human? Why would ... No, I know why. It doesn't take a stretch of the imagination to picture a human or some fanatical group messing with magic they didn't understand, looking for power, thinking alliances could be made with the monsters. We call these beings monsters, which they certainly are, but humans can be just as monstrous.

Vex leans back, crossing their hands behind them. I'm not sure if it's intentional, but the move shows off their chest and abs to perfection. In fact, every move, every gesture they make is graceful, powerful, alluring.

I blink at them as they say, "Well, back to what I was saying before ... What is Easter? I mean, I get the sacrificial thing, and the magically coming back to life. Classic god work there." I chuckle. I'm not religious, and I've never really taken a close look at our holidays, but seeing it from an outside point of view is ... amusing. "But then there's the bunny and candy and eggs. What? And the same goes for Valentine's Day. Again, I get the martyrdom and the romance of the original story, but what's with the cupids and chocolates?"

My chuckle turns to a full-blown laugh. It feels good. I feel lighter. When was the last time I *really* laughed? That question sobers me up, but I keep a soft smile on my lips. "You know, I have no idea. You're right. A lot of our holidays make no sense. I'm sure there's some explanation for it all, but I don't know it."

Vex laughs, the sound surprisingly deep and musical. That simple sound stirs something in me. They shift, scratching the side of their neck, and that draws my attention to their shimmering skin, their gold eyes.

I can't let myself forget they are a monster. I can't relax. I can't afford to lower my guard. That's how you die. I feel my body tensing, and Vex must notice too, because they curl inwards slightly, making themselves even smaller. It's like they are trying to be as unthreatening as possible. Shame spears through me. Vex hasn't done anything to deserve such hateful thoughts from me. They have been ... kind. But if I'm being honest with myself, it's not physical harm I fear. Vex seems to have the power to cut down my emotional defenses. It's not that they are a monster, not really. It's that I'm not ready for *that*. I'm not ready to let go of Reece. I can't.

Keeping their head down, Vex says, "So, Valentine's day ..."

I blink several times, almost physically dizzy from the whiplash of my thoughts. I can't seem to get my footing with Vex. Slowly, they lift their head and look at me with a small smile. Damn it if my cock doesn't kick against my pants at that look. I grip the marble counter so hard, my knuckles turn white. I don't want to feel this way about a monster ... or anyone. I really don't.

Reece's voice cuts through my spinning thoughts. *"Yes, you do. You love love. And that's okay, Max."*

Vex clears their throat. "I only ask because I think, despite the confusing elements, I'd like this holiday very much. Showering the one you care about with gifts, be it extra love and affection, or physical presents sounds ... nice."

It is. Reece gave me the red riding hood painting for Valentine's the year before he ... I gave Reece a new pistol he'd had his eye on for a while. We had a lavish dinner then went hunting. After, we made love, finishing all tangled in the bedding, peppering each other with soft kisses until we fell asleep in each other's arms, his toes pressed to my calf like always.

I'm so used to the burning grief, I don't realize a few tears have escaped until movement brings me out of my memories. Vex's face pulls back in panic, their eyes wide, their forehead furrowed with their hands held up before them. Backing away from me, they whisper, "I'm sorry, Max. I didn't mean to. Forget I asked. Please forgive me. I'm sorry. I'm so sorry. I ..."

I wipe the tears from my face with a frown. How is this *monster* so considerate of my feelings? In the few hours I've spent with Vex, they have shown more regard for me than any of my "relationships" since Reece. Peter even used to get this annoyed look on his face when I'd stare at the painting too long, or god forbid, bring up Reece's name. Was it fair to the men I "dated" that I've been holding onto Reece's memory so tightly? Probably not. Do I care? Also, no. I loved him. And he loved me. How are you supposed to move on from that?

Reece whispers in my mind. *"Moving on doesn't mean forgetting. Go on, take this one little step."* My internal conversations with 'Reece' have become so common, I feel him in every word. I'm well aware that the voice in my head is just my subconscious using my memories of Reece to keep me from fully descending into despair, but I don't care. I like talking to 'him'. It helps me figure things out.

Vex is now at the archway that leads to the dining room. Well, it's more like a dining hall. You could hold full-on banquets in that room. They look everywhere but at me as they say, "Come, let's go sit somewhere more comfortable while we wait for The Divide to fall. There's a really plush sofa in my study." The skin of their cheeks darkens in a flush as they hurriedly continue. "Or the sitting room has many places to lounge." They wave a hand at the small table in the corner of the kitchen, their voice getting higher and their words coming faster. "Or we can just sit there. I can make us a drink. I can fix your favorite. Shit. Sorry. Yes, I know what you like to drink, at least what you seem to like at night before you go to bed." They fall quiet, running a hand through their hair before mumbling, "Sorry. I'm really messing things up here."

Taking a deep breath, I listen to the Reece in my head. I take a step. I cross the room, rounding the large island, my boots making soft thuds on the stone floor. Vex watches me, and for the first time, *I* feel like the predator in the room.

Stopping with just a few inches between us, I take another deep breath. Chocolate. Vex smells like chocolate. They would be my perfect valentine. I allow a little smile to lift my lips. "You know what I like to eat, and my favorite drink. You know about my monster book. You probably know what I wear to bed."

Their blush spreads down their neck, confirming they do know what I sleep in ... nothing. My small smile turns into a grin. "Your stalking game is on point, Vex." I can't help but notice how their gold eyes sparkle. "And, you were right. Valentine's day is a lovely holiday. If you have someone to celebrate with, which I don't as of yesterday. Otherwise, it's terribly lonely."

Their lashes flutter as they look up at me. "So, Peter is ...?"

"Damn, Vex, what don't you know about me? No, Peter and I are no more."

They swallow, their eyes dropping to the floor. They fiddle with the pleats of their kilt. "And ... Reece?"

Hearing his name on Vex's lips doesn't hurt as bad as I thought it would. In fact, something unravels inside me, because Vex's tone wasn't accusing. There was no annoyance or even pity. It feels like they asked about Reece because they really want to know.

I can't dive into the whole story, not right now. I just ... can't. Only a single word tumbles from my mouth. "Gone."

Vex holds my gaze for a long moment before they nod their head. A little smile lifts their pretty cheeks. "But you still love him."

They don't pose it as a question, and I like that. "Yes. I think I always will."

"Good. It's good to hold onto the good things."

I look down at the beautiful starlight monster before me in shock. I know I haven't misread the heat in their eyes. They certainly surrendered beautifully under my kiss. But there's no jealousy in their voice. They don't mind me holding onto the memory of a past love?

Something kicks against my heart. Vex is right. It is good to hold onto the good things in your life. Even if it's gone. I realize in this moment, that me holding on to Reece hasn't been holding me back. His love set the standard for me, and I won't settle for less even if that means dying alone.

And I'm okay with that.

Vex moves, grabbing two glasses from a cabinet. When they hold them up, a brow raised, I answer their silent question. "Just water is fine."

They nod, filling both glasses before handing one to me. I take a sip. It's cool and refreshing. I stare into my cup as I attempt to shift my preconceptions of the monster realm ... and my monster.

Vex shifts, and I raise my gaze to find them watching me. They smile. "You're thinking pretty hard over there."

I look around the kitchen, waving a hand. "It's all just so ..."

"Normal?" I nod, and they set their drink down with a little clinking sound. "Let me guess, you thought our realm would be all chaos, sulfur choking the air, screams rending the night, monsters lurking in forests and swamps?"

My cheeks heat with embarrassment as I shrug. They wave me off with a chuckle. "It's okay. The more animalistic monsters do live in the wilds. But most of us live like this."

"And it's all done with magic?"

Vex nods. "Yes. Magic is *everything* here. Without it, you don't last long. It's equivalent to human technology and currency all in one."

I look around again, taking in the opulent kitchen. "So, this house was built with magic?"

"Yes. My magic to be precise."

"And what if your magic depletes or you die? Will all this crumble to the ground?"

They shake their head, sending their black hair swaying over their eyes. "No. Let's see how to put this ... It's like the magic is like a construction worker. Your house didn't collapse when the people who built it left."

I guess that makes sense. Cracking my knuckles, I voice the uncomfortable thought poking at my brain. "So, since magic is so important, and you say human souls or whatever are pretty potent ... and we are easier prey than going after other monsters for their magic ... Humans are nothing more than a natural resource to you all."

There's a long pause, but Vex answers, "Yes."

I nod, surprised at the lack of outrage I feel at that confession. I mean, the whole situation is fucked up, but humans do the same thing. We invade, we conquer, we exploit ... all because we want more than what we have.

Before I realized it, hours passed as we talked, standing in their kitchen like it's something we've done together for years.

Eventually, a companionable silence falls between us. Vex fiddles with the pleats of their kilt, the move so adorable, it pulls at something in my heart. I take a step, crowding Vex. With them embraced by my shadow, they are the deepest shade of night with sparkling constellations swirling across their skin. They are so beautiful.

And they are strong, protective, and considerate ... towards me anyway. And fuck if I'm not feeling selfish right now. I've lost a lot over the years, including myself. Right now, I just *want.* But overpowering the ache of desire is the need to know ...

Leaning over them, I brace my hands on the counter on either side of them, lowering my voice as I say, "Vex, is it the blood? Your blood that's making me feel this way?"

They shake their head, their lips pressed tightly together. There's something in their eyes, like they want to say something. My free hand slips around their throat, not squeezing, just ... holding. Their pupils dilate, and I stare at their lips as I ask, "Why have you been showing up behind my house every night since Christmas? Why have you been watching me? What are we to each other?"

CHAPTER

VEX

Words. Why can't I find any words? My brain is stuck on the fact that Max is so very close. I can smell the vegetables and vinegar on his breath. Should I tell him we're mates? I want to tell him. Up until now, I've been content with watching, waiting. But now that I've touched him, conversed with him, now that I know for sure that he's mine ... Fuck, he kissed me after I fought Jarius for him, and it was fucking sexy.

Max backs away, taking his delicious heat with him, but when I look at his face, it's pulled in a grimace of discomfort. He clutches his chest. "Why did it just get colder?"

I tilt my head, looking to see if the door was left open. It's shut tight. Snapping my head back towards Max, I ask, "Cold on the outside or inside?"

He takes a stuttering breath. "Inside."

I send tendrils of my magic outwards, testing, feeling.

Sure enough, The Divide is weakening. It's about to fall. With a blur of motion, I move to Max, gripping his shoulder. "Try not to resist it. You must have bled enough. The Divide is pulling you back to the human realm. The magic puts everything back in its place. Monsters who try to linger in the human realm are forcefully returned to the monster realm. And it looks like the magic knows you don't belong here." My heart squeezes as I say those words. Max does belong. He belongs with me.

I focus back on him. "Try to breathe. It's worse if you fight it."

He groans. "How do I not fight it? It hurts." His bright, pain-filled eyes find mine. "Does it hurt this much every time you cross between our worlds?"

"I've learned not to resist. Or better yet, I cross back over before the magic of The Divide starts to go back up." I move closer to Max, my blood racing when he doesn't object to my nearness. "But I've found myself lingering in the human realm much longer than I should, because ..."

Max is trembling under my touch. I wrap my free hand around the one that's gripping his shirt over his chest and blurt out, "The reason I've come to your house every night is because you are mine, Max. My mate. You and I are fated."

He tenses slightly, but at least he doesn't pull away as he says, "Mates. Like *soulmates*? Like in stories?" I nod, and he frowns. "That's nonsense. Why would a human and monster be fated? What if The Divide had never fallen? What if we'd never met? Were we supposed to go through life without the other half of our soul?" I'm shocked he understands soul bonds so well, but he's getting angrier with each word. "We don't even live in the same realms. Six hours, Vex. Six hours each day, or turn, or whatever you call it. That ... we can't be ..."

I look into his eyes. "But, Max, The Divide did fall. We have met. Doesn't that say something about fate?"

He shakes his head, his trembling getting worse. "I had a great love. He was my everything. When he died"—Max's eyes harden—"no, when he was *taken* from me by a *monster*, I almost didn't survive it."

Sorrow scoops out my belly. Of course it wasn't an accident or illness that killed his Reece. It was a monster who took Max's love from him ... and that guts me.

Max's eyes pinch at the corners. "Fuck, the cold ... it's like it's ..."

"Pulling at you from the inside out. I know, Max. Breathe."

He dips his head, but not before I see his teeth clench. His voice comes out as a harsh whisper. "No. This can't be right. You must be mistaken." His eyes snap back to mine, and the angry fire there nearly has me stumbling back. "If this"—He waves a hand between us—"is fated, then our feelings are fabricated." Max's voice starts to get louder. "What I feel for you can't be real. Fate means neither of us has a choice." He slaps his chest, his face turning red. "Are you really okay with that? Forced to feel so deeply? How can you be okay with that?"

Okay with it? For monsters, it's what we all hope for—to find our true match in life. But humans, they cling to fleeting emotions, labeling even the smallest of stirrings as love. If only Max would let us, he could experience a true bond of souls and hearts. Not some *thing* of fiction or fantasy. Yes, it may be a form of magic, but that's what love is. Magic.

I press my hand over my chest. "Max, I'd never force you. What being fated means is that I was made to compliment you, and you me. We are a pair."

"Like shoes."

My lips twitch with a smile despite the seriousness of our conversation. "Sure. We are a pair of shoes. But you can still get around just fine with mismatched shoes. You ..." The next words physically hurt to say. "You can choose your path, Max. It doesn't have to include me, but please know, you are always safe with me. Body and heart. No matter what."

His gaze flicks between my lips and my eyes. For just a moment, the softness comes back to his eyes, but then he hunches over with a grunt of pain. "It's all too much. I can't!"

Max disappears.

Fuck. The Divide. I can't follow him from here.

Moving fast, I nearly shatter the kitchen door as I speed out of the house. My bare feet skid on the gravel as I come to a stop. With the cold outside air brushing my skin, I press through the magic that separates the human and monster realms. One blink, and I'm back on the narrow street outside Max's house.

Was he shocked to find himself in his living room, when the moment before he was in my kitchen? Will he be angry when he realizes our homes are literally layered over each other? These past few weeks, I've gotten some small comfort knowing he could be wandering the same space as me, just in a different realm.

In a daze, my feet carry me towards the steps leading to his back door. I've never dared to come this close, and my heart races. I can't hear Max inside, but unless he ran screaming into the night as soon as he crossed over, he's still in there. Step by step, I climb until I'm on the little stoop, the magic of the blood carvings in the threshold humming in warning. I stare at the base of the door, wondering if I could survive crossing them?

Adrenaline spikes through me as the door flies open.

I'm so startled, my skin goes slick for a moment before I pull back my magic. Max glowers at me from his little kitchen. "Your fucking house! You live right here?"

I nod, fiddling with the pleats of my kilt. "That's why I couldn't immediately follow you. Your blood carvings keep me out, even from my realm."

He snaps out his arm, and though his movements look slow to me, I know he's moving quickly for a human. Like the two times before, his hand wraps around my throat, and before I can brace myself, Max yanks me towards him. Towards the barrier. "And you're going to tell me this is fate?"

The front of my body barely scrapes along the magical wall of his blood-carvings. Pain scorches my skin like I was struck by a unicorn's horn. A scream rips from my mouth, but quickly turns to a mewl of agony as the edges of my vision go dark. Max's deep, gravelly voice lifts me from the fog of pain. "This *bond* between us ... will I die if I kill you right now?"

I clear my throat, feeling it bob against his palm. "N-no."

I'm shaky and dizzy, losing consciousness quickly. I can save myself. I'm stronger than him. All I have to do ...

"Fight back!" Max's voice rumbles with rage and confusion and ... "Drug me, flash your eyes, use your strength, your claws, something!"

All I can manage is a weak shake of my head. Max growls, then the sound turns into a scream as he shoves me back, releasing me. My body lurches, my heels falling over the edge of the top step. Before I know it, I'm tumbling down the concrete. It feels like there are a thousand steps instead of just the eight. The pain from the blood-carving barrier still echoes across my skin, a headache thudding behind my eyes.

Two, then three, then two of Max storm down the stairs. I blink, trying to focus. I realize I can't hear the sound of his boots striking the concrete. Opening my mouth, I try to pop my ears. A little whisper of sound comes through as Max crouches in front of me. He grabs my hair, more pain scraping along my scalp as he lifts my head. He thrusts his other arm at me, and while I'm expecting a strike, I don't flinch. I give in. I surrender to the fates and to my mate.

Max's grip gets tighter as he shakes me by my hair. "You see this?" The back of his forearm nearly brushes my nose. "All these marks. Every single x is a kill, a monster that died by my hand."

I blink at the marks. There are a lot. Well over a dozen. Maybe over twenty. I'm still too dizzy to count. But I don't care. In fact ...

My gaze climbs to Max's face. His mouth is tight with anger, but the slight pinching around his eyes shows his desperation. I must be gentle with my mate. Patient.

I attempt a smile. "Impressive."

Max reels back, his eyes widening for a second before they harden once more. Shaking me again, he growls. "Didn't you hear what I said? I've killed monsters. A lot of them. I *hate* monsters. They just keep coming, keep killing. They killed Reece!"

I feel his anger and sadness to my bones. Everything hurts. The magic of the blood-carvings is strong, and it's taking longer for me to heal myself. As silence descends, I send out my magic, making sure we are alone in this narrow street behind my mate's house. I'll give him time, but if there's danger, I'll have to act.

The only monster I feel is Paine, the dremar who lives with his human mate across the street. There's no violence in his magic, so we're under no threat from him right now. In fact, he feels ... content, happy. I look up at Max with so much longing in my heart, it hurts. Will he ever accept me? Accept us?

Focusing on the large male before me, I hold his gaze. I won't apologize for Reece. I didn't do it. Instead, I try to offer understanding. "I know, Max. I know. Humans were at the top of the hierarchy for so long. But as your species is known to do, you've adapted well to becoming prey once more. You've found a way to protect yourselves." I smile. "You fight back."

His grip finally loosens until it's just a deliciously firm tug on my hair. Struggling to focus, I go on. "And Max, I've killed monsters too. I killed one just yesterday right here, remember? You saw."

His eyes skip between mine, and for a second, I think he's calmed down a little, but then he shakes his head. He releases me so suddenly, I barely keep my head from thumping on the street. He points to an x on his arm closer to his elbow. "This one. This was one of your kind. An anza. I didn't know what it was called. Didn't care."

Propping myself on my forearm, I raise my brows. "How?"

He blinks at me, his mouth opening, then closing before saying. "Shot it through the head."

"Impressive. Anza, as you have seen, are extremely fast. That is quite remarkable."

Max huffs. Moving slowly, I point to another x on his muscled forearm. "And this one?"

There's a long pause before he answers. "One of those thin, bony monsters with the wide horns like tree branches."

I nod. "Sounds like a quilen. They move through shadows. How'd you kill it?"

"Sliced the tendons on the back of its legs then ... again, shot it in the head."

With the barest of touches, I press my finger to another x. "This one?"

"One of those, what did you call it? Jotune?"

"Joteunn. The werewolf creature?"

Max nods. "Yeah. Blinded it with acid, then cut off its head and ripped out its heart."

"You are quite knowledgeable"—I'm unable to keep the growl of pride and desire out of my voice—"and lethal." My finger still rests on his arm, and the fact he hasn't pulled away gives me hope. I've healed myself, so I'm feeling steadier, physically anyway. As slowly as I can so as not to spook Max, I shift to sit, crossing my legs under my kilt. "Are there any monsters you need more information on?"

"What?"

"Information. On monsters. All you have to do is ask." When he doesn't say anything, I point at myself. "Stalker, remember? You were a hunter. I know about your monster book." I glance at his tattoos before meeting his gaze once more.

All he says is, "I don't go on hunts anymore."

We both fall silent, and the only sound is the occasional scrape of his boot on the pavement when he shifts in his crouched position. After a few minutes, he sighs, pressing his hands to his thighs, standing. He looms over me. It would be intimidating if it wasn't so sexy. Cocking his head, he asks, "You okay?"

I nod as I pinch the leather pleats of my kilt. Seems I may have talked my mate down from his panic.

He grunts, spinning around. "Stay there for a second."

With practiced moves, he flips up a cover to a panel

next to his garage and punches in a code. Slowly and silently, the wide door lifts, and Max disappears inside. A large black vehicle sits in the shadows. It has huge tires, the body is reinforced, and there's a roof rack sitting on top, empty but ready to go.

A few seconds later, Max comes out holding a large jug.

Bleach?

His long strides take him up the steps to his still open back door. I leap to my feet, and I'm at his side in a flash. I don't touch the barrier, but it hisses and sparks in warning. I do my best to ignore it, focusing on my mate. "What are you doing, Max?"

He shakes the container. "Isn't it obvious? Now stand back. Don't want to burn that pretty skin."

His jaw flexes as he bites the inside of his cheek. I don't think he meant to say that out loud, but fuck, I'm glad he did. He thinks my skin is pretty. Max thinks my deadly skin is pretty.

I back up, descending to the second step and watch as Max dumps the bleach on his threshold. It's goopier than I thought it would be. I expected the liquid to splash, but what comes out of the jug is more like slime that splats onto the carvings. Pausing, Max shakes the container, and I can hear a little bit of the bleach sloshing around. Jerking his head towards his door, he says, "Come see if that's enough."

Climbing back up the stairs, my heart races in anticipation. Max is inviting me into his home. This is surreal. After all these weeks, I never thought I'd be where I am right now. As I get closer, I brace for the magic to hit me, but ... nothing. Lifting a hand, I take a breath and shove my arm through the open doorway. Again, nothing.

I almost jump as Max says, "Seems okay. Come on then."

He shoves past me, our arms brushing. I follow him into his kitchen, where I've watched him night after night. And now I'm here. With a soft thud, Max sets the bleach bottle on the counter. Digging his hand into his waistband, he draws out his gun still in its little case. I fight the urge to flinch. He's shot at me enough these past few hours.

Max doesn't shoot. He pulls the gun out of its case; I think it's called a holder. No, a holster. Then Max pushes a button that has the piece of the gun that holds the bullets sliding out. He checks something, looking in the weapon before he sets everything on the counter. Turning, Max leans back, crossing his arms. "So, this is my place. Welcome, I guess."

Everything in me strains to go to him, to wrap my arms around him and hug my thanks. But I just nod, feeling my cheeks heat with my blush. "Thank you, Max."

He's so still, just watching me. I'm afraid to do anything that might break this calm truce we've reached, but my protective instincts are making me sweat. I turn, closing the kitchen door. Pressing my hand to the cream painted wood, I let my magic pour out. It floods into the wood, the plaster, the steel, the glass ... until a strong ward encases the entire house.

Max looks around, up at the ceiling, then back at me. "What did you just do?"

"Warded your house. After what happened at my place"—my eyes flick to his wrist where he'd sliced himself open—"I don't think it wise for you to bleed again to repower your carvings."

He shrugs. "I wasn't worried about it. If a monster tries to get in, I'll handle it."

Fear and anger skips through my heart. No, he won't. Not while I'm around.

His bicep flexes as he reaches up and rubs the back of his neck. Dropping his arm, he cracks his knuckles one at a time before sighing. Without a word, he shoves off the counter and strides down the dark hallway. He doesn't go two steps before slamming his hand against a switch. Light fills the hall, and I see his shoulders relax just a bit before he continues walking.

My mate is definitely not fond of the dark.

I'm not sure if he wants me to follow, but I do. I glance at the large painting on the wall to my left. It's dark and beautiful. And in the center of the painting is my mate. He's broad and strong, the muscles of his back straining as he walks down the path with monsters closing in on him from the shadows. It's breathtaking. Max doesn't even glance at it.

My steps are silent as I enter a small but cozy living room. He bends over, causing my blood to race as he clicks on a lamp. Kneeling before a cold fireplace, Max begins to stack wood, but before he reaches for the tube labeled matches, I touch his back. When he looks up at me over his shoulder, my breath catches in my lungs for a moment. He's so ... perfect.

I nod at the logs. "May I?"

His brows furrow, but he nods. Flicking some of my magic outward, the wood catches fire, quickly warming the small space. I rub my fingers. I've used a lot of magic in the last few hours. I'm not depleted, but I'm getting close.

Max stands, towering over me. He crowds my space, and

I gladly let him. Stepping forward, his boots bump my toes, and I back up a step. He does it again, and I back up again. Max stalks me until the back of my legs hit a piece of furniture. I tumble back, landing on a soft sofa. Leaning over me, he places a hand on the back of the couch, enveloping me.

Could I get out from under him? Of course. Do I move a single muscle? No. I barely breathe as Max stares at my face. A small frown pulls at his lips, his blue eyes softening slightly as he says, "I know I've been running hot and cold here. I'm sure I'm giving you whiplash. I'm making myself dizzy with my seesawing emotions."

I don't know what a seesaw is, but I understand what he's saying.

Max goes on. "I just ... I'm having a hard time reconciling being angry over my feelings for you and at the same time ..."

I dare to whisper, "You feel drawn to me."

He nods, his eyes never leaving mine. At least he doesn't seem afraid I'll use my hypnosis through my eyes. Licking my lips, I ask, "Is there anything I can do to help?"

His gaze drops to my mouth, and my cock kicks against my kilt as he says, "Maybe."

Whatever he asks of me is his.

I notice his fingers trembling slightly as he reaches for my hand. Taking my wrist, he wraps my arm behind my back. It's a little awkward, but I don't resist. He moves my other hand to do the same, then he easily cuffs both my wrists with one of his large hands. He holds me captive as he braces one knee on the sofa, brushing my outer thigh.

I can't breathe. My pulse is racing so fast, I can hear it beating in my ears. *Kiss me. Please.*

His arm flexes, gripping the back of the sofa harder until it groans. I know there's desire and longing in my eyes, and I hope he can see it. I also hope he sees that he can trust me. He may have a good grip on my arms behind my back, but we both know I could easily get out of his hold if I wanted. But I don't. I won't. I let Max have all the control.

After a moment, he bends over, his lips aimed right for mine.

Fuck, finally.

CHAPTER 10

MAX

What am I doing?

"Giving in, sweetheart."

Vex licks their lips, their gaze slipping to the bulge in my pants, and my cock gets harder at the thought of Vex scraping their fangs lightly across my shaft. The image of them sucking me deep until I hit the back of their throat does things to me. Vex is the perfect size, small and muscular, delicate and strong. Perfect. It really is like they were made for me.

That thought snaps a thread of anger through me. I don't like the idea of fate or magic or whatever controlling how I feel, who I'm supposed to be with.

Reece's voice tsks at me. *"Quit holding back, you stubborn bastard. What do you know of magic or fate? What if this is the real deal? Let yourself hope. Let yourself believe. Let yourself love again."*

Can I?

As Vex's eyes hold my gaze, I realize, yes, maybe I can.

I close the distance between us. Their lips are soft, yielding. They melt under me, their soft moan curling low in my belly. My tongue brushes the seam of their mouth, and they open. The heat of their mouth caresses me, and I'm overwhelmed by their vanilla and chocolate scent. So sweet, so dark.

They flex, trying to roll their hips towards me, but they don't pull from the hold I have on their wrists. I know Vex could easily escape me, but they don't. They submit. Beautifully.

I release the back of the couch, my need to touch them driving my movements. My hand cups their face, and I'm shocked at my own gentleness. Angling Vex's face, I take our kiss deeper with a growl of need. My fingers explore, caressing the shell of their ear, drawing a whimper from them that I swallow greedily. I want to linger here at their sensitive ear and see what other reactions I can get from them. My tongue follows the path of my fingers, then I nip their lobe. They gasp, and it's so beautiful.

Wrapping my hand behind their neck, I breathe them in. They feel so good, so perfect, just as I imagined their starlight skin would feel.

I want more. I *need* more.

As if reading my thoughts, Vex pulls back, their breaths coming fast, their chest rising quickly as they pant. "Max. My Max. Please. Please let me ..."

I'm not sure what they're asking for, but just hearing them call me theirs has my heart melting. I've missed being someone's someone. I never felt that from Peter, or anyone since Reece. My body freezes when the usual pang of despair doesn't hit me at the thought of Reece. I realize there's room inside me for Reece's love as well as something new. Being needed again has given me back a piece of myself.

My fingers trace Vex's face, and there's such longing in their gold eyes, I can't help but fall. In this moment, I don't see a monster, I see someone who has the potential to be not only good to me, but good *for* me. Vex is obviously stronger than me, despite our size difference, plus they have magic. But still, they let me have control. They let me lead. They give me what I need without me having to say it. Is this what being fated means?

"Max." Vex's voice is soft, drawing my gaze back to their face. They look at me with that longing once more, then their eyes dip to my obvious erection.

Gripping the back of their neck, I release their wrists. "Undo my pants."

Vex swallows, hands flying to do as I commanded. As soon as my zipper is down, they reach for the waistband of my briefs, but I move. With a twist of my body, I switch our positions, shoving Vex to their knees. Their hands land on my thighs, their fingers trembling. I lift my hips, and they comply with my silent order. Gripping my pants and briefs together, Vex slides them down to my ankles. The fabric bunches around my boots, but when they go to unlace them, I pull their face towards my aching cock.

As Vex's breath feathers over my length, it kicks with anticipation. I can't believe that my little monster has so thoroughly unraveled me.

Maybe there is something to this mate thing if it feels this good ... this right.

Reece's voice doesn't answer me, but I see his smile in my mind.

With their hungry gold eyes on my cock, Vex whispers, "I can't believe ..." Their mouth opens and they swallow me to the hilt. I slide down their throat, and a groan rumbles from my chest.

Fuck me. "So good. Yes, Vex."

I'm shocked how sinful their name sounds coming from my mouth, but I like it. They moan then swallow, constricting around me. As they pull back, pleasure tingles over my body at the sight of their saliva coating my cock. I move my hand from their neck to grip their hair. Vex's moan deepens as I tug softly, pulling them back down my length until their nose brushes my blond curls along my lower belly. One of their hands grips my thigh as the other cups my balls.

It feels so good. My head starts to fall back against the couch, but the need to watch Vex is stronger. I keep my eyes on them as I control their pace. Saliva drips over my balls, and the wet slurping sound of their mouth taking me deep over and over fills the room.

Pressure builds. Every time I hit the back of Vex's throat, a grunt punches from my mouth. I'm so close, but ... I want more. I want ... connection. I pull them off my cock, and a string of spit drips from their lips. It's so insanely sexy, I can't help myself. Lunging forward, I crash my mouth to theirs, devouring my taste from their lips.

Vex's groan turns to a growl, and when I open my eyes, I yank them away from me. "What the fuck, Vex!"

Their skin is glowing. I wait for the hallucinations to hit, but when nothing happens, I search Vex's face. Their teeth worry at their bottom lip as they say, "I'm sorry, Max. Here, feel." They take my hand, and I only resist a little as they bring my fingers to their chest. "See, dry. No secretions. This glow is ... It's harmless, just a bodily reaction to my need."

I get the feeling Vex is leaving something out about

what's happening to them. My fingers trail up their chest and across their shoulder. True to their word, even though the blue-black glow intensifies, their skin is dry. I take a deep breath of rich chocolate. Letting my gaze travel over their body, I swallow, my cock throbbing with need. My deep voice rumbles a command. "Touch yourself, Vex."

Vex's eyes fill with dark desire as they stroke their hand down my cock once, gathering their saliva. They raise their hand to their mouth, and suck three of their fingers between their lips, their eyes holding my gaze. They are sex incarnate. Everything in me wants to pin them to the floor and sink into them until we are one, body and soul. I want Vex to mewl and groan and scream under me. I want to feel them squeeze and shutter around me as they come apart with my cock deep inside them. I want them to hold me tight. I want them to fall asleep on my chest.

Fuck. I'm in trouble.

I pull my shirt off, tossing it behind the couch as I watch Vex. I expect them to reach for their cock, but instead, a whiff of leather combines with their sweet scent as Vex reaches back, flipping up their kilt. Two of their fingers slide inside their ass, the wet sound vulgar and erotic.

"Fuck, Vex, yes. Work yourself for me. Prepare yourself." I grip my cock, and their eyes greedily watch as I stroke myself. "You want this?" Vex adds a third finger on their next thrust, nodding. I have to squeeze my dick to keep from coming as I say, "Then get that hole nice and stretched and wet for me."

Their head dives for me, swallowing my cock before pulling back to swirl their tongue around my head. Jesus fucking Christ. My monster knows how to give head. Vex only sucks me for a few more strokes before I pull them off. "Fuck, Vex. I'm so close, but I want you."

"Yes, fuck, Max. Please."

The way they beg for me has my head spinning. Grabbing their shoulders, I pull them onto my lap, their kilt fanning around our hips. I want to see them, but before I can reach for the fabric, Vex holds up their hand, palm up. "May I?" Raising a brow, I cock my head, and they smile. Damn, they are so beautiful. "The hallucinogen isn't the only thing I can secrete." Their palm goes slick, and they rub their delicate fingers together. "This is ... how can I explain? I guess it's like a pleasure lubricant. It'll feel good, I promise." My cock kicks against their ass cheeks as they meet and hold my gaze. "You will still be in control, Max. Nothing mind altering. Just a little heat and a lot of pleasure."

"Show me." With an agonizingly slow, tight stroke, Vex pumps their fist down my cock. I can't keep my eyes from rolling back, and my head thunks against the back of the couch. "Fuuuuck, Vex."

Their lips caress my neck. A wet stripe follows their tongue as they lick me with a breathy whisper, "I know, Max."

A few more strokes send bliss racing through my blood. It feels like every hair on my body stands on end. My skin prickles, and pre-cum leaks from my cock. Vex grinds back against me, and I grip their hips. "Get on my cock, now, Vex."

The lube on their hand thickens, slurping with the pumping motion of their hand. With a flex of their thighs, they rise, lining my head up at their entrance. The edges of my vision sparkle with little white stars as Vex starts to lower onto me.

When I breach the tight ring of their ass, I lose it.

Gripping their hips, I slam them down my length, filling them with one brutal thrust. We both groan as Vex throws their head back, mouth open, throat exposed. Vex's skin glows like a dark star. If love had a look, this would be it.

Holding them in place, I grind my hips. I know I've brushed a sensitive place inside them when their eyes widen on a silent gasp. I don't know if Vex has a prostate, but whatever I've hit does it for them. My fingers dig harder into their hips as I try to keep myself from rutting up into them. I hold still as I ask, "You okay?"

Vex lowers their head to look at me, and a second later, their lips press to mine. Our tongues dance, and I'm swept away by the passion between us, enjoying the heat of them holding me deep inside them. When they pull back, there's desperation in their bright eyes and shaky breath. "Please, Max. Fuck me."

My hands move and flex against their ass cheeks. There's a beat of silence, then I dig my boots into the floor. I lift Vex until just the tip of my cock is inside them, then I snap my hips up as I pull them down, hard. Over and over, my cock weeps, throbs, aches as I fuck into the monster on my lap.

My monster. Mine.

I'm going to come. Vex is so tight, so wet, their lubrication tingling over my length and across my balls. I feel like I'm floating, my skin being caressed by wisps of starlight. It's almost painful.

With a growl, I flip the front of Vex's kilt up, tucking it behind their dick. I keep thrusting and grinding my cock inside them as I look my fill. Their shaft is darker than the rest of them, pearlescent cum dripping from their swollen tip. As I watch, their length starts to glisten wetly with their lube secretion. I wonder what it tastes like, the mix of their cum and the pleasure lube? I'll find out later.

Wrapping my fist around their cock, I stroke them, eliciting a lovely moan from their lips. I squeeze tighter, running my thumb over their slit, rolling my palm around their head before sliding back to their base. The contrast of their dark, glowing skin against my pale hand mesmerizes me. Their head falls back again, exposing the column of their throat, and I have the sudden urge to bite them, to claim them, to mark them, to destroy them until I am all they want.

Between the two of us right now, I am the monster.

My thrusts get faster as my climax draws closer. Our bodies slap together, the sound mixing with our panting, grunting breaths. I pump my tight fist up and down Vex's cock as I say, "This beautiful cock is mine, Vex. Come for me. Paint my chest while I fill your ass until you're leaking with my seed."

With beautiful obedience, Vex shouts my name to the ceiling as they come. Thick ribbons of cum land on my chest and stomach. With one more violent thrust, stars burst in my vision, my scalp tingles, and my body trembles with my release. I don't know that I've ever come so hard.

Pleasure continues to spark low in my belly as my cum starts to drip out of Vex and onto my thighs. Their cock is still twitching in my fist, their cum mixing with the lube and our sweat. They lean in, their chocolate scent surrounding me. They lick my throat, then before I know what's happening, their teeth gently close around the flesh where my shoulder meets my neck without breaking the skin. With a surprised grunt, I come again, my hips bucking into Vex, my cock pulsing with each pleasured spurt of my cum.

They release their bite, then lick me again before collapsing on my chest.

Our breaths slow. Our sweat dries. I'm still inside Vex, their inner muscles flexing around me every now and then. Their breath fans across my chest, and I realize my fingers are combing through their hair then running down their back. Vex is still glowing.

I smile, pressing a kiss to the top of their head, nuzzling my nose in their soft hair. Right now, I don't give a shit about fate or gods. All I care about is the sweet, considerate, brave monster in my arms. Vex sees me, and I think I'm starting to really see them.

A giddy little thought dances through my head. What would Vex say if I asked them to be my Valentine? They asked earlier. It might be fun showing them all the tacky, fun, sweet, romantic ways to celebrate. I close my eyes, breathing them in.

If only to myself and to the Reece that lives in my mind, I admit that I like Vex. A lot.

CHAPTER

VEX

I jolt awake as the icy magic of The Divide wraps around me. Blinking my eyes, I try to remember where I am. I don't recall the last time I slept, like fully slept. I rest. I take breaks, but I don't sleep. I don't need to.

Sitting back, I realize I'm sore. My thighs ache from sleeping spread around ... Max! We ...

I drink in his body, his chest rising and falling with an easy rhythm. He's no softer in sleep than he is awake—like he could leap up at any moment and be ready for action. His blond lashes fan over his cheeks, his mouth parted slightly. He's just so ...

My chest itches, and when I rub my fingers over my skin, little flakes of dried cum fall to the pleats of my kilt. More of my cum decorates Max's chest as well. I like it. I've marked him in that small way. Mine. My human. My mate.

The Divide pulls at me again, and the burn is so

intense I can't keep the gasp from escaping my mouth. Max's eyes blink open. He winces as he lifts his head off the back of the sofa. With a groan, he rubs his neck, rolling his head as he grumbles, "Ouch. I'm too old to sleep like that. What ...?"

His sleepy blue eyes land on me, his other hand flexing at the top of my thigh where it was resting. Max blinks a few times, looks around as if taking stock of his surroundings, then his head whips back to me. "Shit. I shouldn't have—"

Pain lances up my hip as I bounce off my kitchen island and land on my ass on the floor. I'm back in the monster realm. I glower at my ceiling, at my house, at the monster realm as a whole. What have I done for the fates to punish me so?

Max's last words before The Divide pulled me back here echo through my mind. *"I shouldn't have ..."* What? Kissed me? Fucked me? Is he pacing his house, berating himself for what happened? Will his anger build throughout the turn? Will he keep himself barricaded in his house when The Divide goes back down? Is it over between us before it even begins?

No. I won't believe it. I won't jump to conclusions. We are meant to be together. I'll figure out how to fix things. Somehow.

Grabbing the edge of the counter, I pull myself up, unbuckling my kilt. I start to mull over some ideas on how I can reassure my mate as I lay out the leather garment next to the sink. I tap into my magic, forgetting for a moment how depleted I am. Well, fuck. Guess I have to clean it by hand. I don't bother lighting the floating orbs in the room, saving what little magic I have left.

I work some soap into a lather and run a cloth over my kilt as I worry at my lip. Max and I ... last night was more than I could have imagined. And I've imagined *a lot*. His lips, his hands, his cock. I had convinced myself that I'd be content with anything Max would give me, but now that I've had him, experienced his touch, his kiss, his … I am decidedly *not* content. I want more. I want all of him, all of the time.

But those words, *I shouldn't have …*

I look down at the spreading puddle on my kilt. I stopped wiping it in my distraction, and now it's a wet mess. Quickly, I use a dry cloth to mop up the excess water, then continue to gently wash the leather. Once done, I lay it on a large towel to finish drying so I can apply the conditioner.

Without really meaning to, I find myself standing in my back hall. I look down at my bare feet and wiggle my toes against the polished wood. Right here is where Max stands in his kitchen. This is where he watches me every night as I watch him. This is where he let me into his home last night.

My shoulders pinch, and I run my hands through my hair. Not only am I maintaining the wards on my house, but I'm also still holding the wards around Max's house. I'd let my personal wards fall in a heartbeat if it meant protecting my mate. But I won't let it come to that.

Pushing through my door, I take a deep breath of the cold air. Adjusting my body heat, I move down the path, past my gardens with their artificial sunlight orbs. They flicker, a sign of how low my magic reserves are—magic I need to grow my garden. Max loves his vegetables, and I love my flowers.

With a burst of speed, I exit my grounds, scenting the air, scanning my surroundings for a monster to hunt. I need magic. Lots of it. As I run, the air caresses my skin. It's freeing being completely bare, but I do miss my kilt. I miss the slide of the leather over my skin. Funny, I spent years without a stitch of clothing, never even thinking about it. With a smile, I push myself faster, embracing the thrill of the hunt.

A small pack of hellhounds tries to keep pace with me for a while, each of us sizing the other up. I sense their hunger, but they keep their distance. After a few more strides, they back off, and I let them go. They'd be more trouble than they are worth. I'd have to kill all of them to regain even a fraction of the magic I need.

I pass a quilen, recalling the story Max told me of how he took one of those monsters down. My mate is quite the warrior. A warrior who, right now, might be regretting the most beautiful night of my life. Damn it.

Slowing, I press my hand to my chest, over my aching heart. What if Max rejects me? What will I do if he doesn't want me? What if ... he tries to kill me again? I know I won't be able to hurt him. Do I ... do I try to stay away? Leave him alone?

A bite of pain shoots up my foot as I stumble at the thought. I stand still, hand pressed to my chest, gaze lifted to the dark sky. Little puffs of white mist rise from my mouth with every exhale. "How am I supposed to just leave my mate?"

Shaking my head, I try to bolster my determination. I recall the sadness in his eyes, the desperation on his face when he showed me his tattoos. He was not only trying to scare me away, he was trying to remind himself why he should hate me. And maybe he should. Maybe we should hate each other. He was a monster hunter, after all.

But—and maybe I'm just seeing what I want to see in Max—it also seemed like he was begging to be seen, to be heard, to be loved.

My skin prickles in warning a split second before the

ground shakes behind me. I don't have to turn to know what beast just landed. I can feel their magic. A nepha. Fuck. Their magic would sustain me for a really, really long time. But ...

"Why are you just standing out here, little anza?" Their voice is like a melody, soft yet commanding. My skin shifts, the oil-slick color deepening as my defenses leak from my pores. My body instinctively knows the threat that's standing behind me, and my nails lengthen to claws, even knowing they will be useless against the tough skin of the nepha.

I turn, taking in the ethereal creature. The nepha smiles at me, his eyes on my nose to avoid my gaze. There's no warmth there, only cruel amusement. His metallic gold wings flare out before he tucks them to his back. Long golden hair frames his delicate face, then spills over one shoulder in a ponytail. His skin glistens as if it's dusted with gold powder.

I shift to the balls of my feet. I should run. Nepha are powerful, as close to the top of the monster food chain one can be without being an ancient. But the ancients don't come out much anymore, so the nepha are it.

He licks his lips, his gold wings flaring once more. "Your magic is depleted, anza. Are you thinking of taking mine?"

Max's face flashes through my mind. I don't care if he thinks what we did was a mistake. I don't care if he rejects me. I'll still protect him at all costs. He's mine, my mate, mine to care for. And to do that, I need magic.

I answer the nepha's question with a question of my own. "Will you barter with me?" He laughs. Guess that answers that. I look the nepha up and down. "Why did you even bother to dirty your pretty feet by landing here?

My tiny reserve of magic would be like a drop of water in the ocean to you."

He shifts his weight to one hip, waving a graceful hand in dismissal. "True, but every morsel counts, doesn't it." His hair floats around him on a magical wind. His wings fully spread as he starts to glow. The humans named these creatures angels, and for good reason. They are so devastatingly beautiful, it is easy to imagine a god forming them with their own hands.

The glow of his body coalesces over his chest, and only because I've seen this before, I'm able to move in time to avoid the blast of golden light that spears right for my head. My eyes burn with the wisps of my magic as I try to make eye contact with the nepha, but it evades me. I'm going to have to get closer. Much closer.

With a blur of movement, I reach for the creature's spread wing. He laughs, snapping his feathers back, the metallic edges tearing deep into my palm. I hiss in pain as my black blood drips to the ground. The nepha simply steps out of reach before shooting another bolt of light at me. This one singes my shoulder, and I press my bleeding hand to the wound.

Do I use my magic to heal myself, or reserve it?

Deciding to hold off on healing myself for now, I move to attack again. The nepha flaps his wings, dodging my reach, and I flash to follow him. We're caught in a dance. I catch another feather on my cheek, and as I rear back from the sting of the deep cut, the nepha's fist rams into the other side of my face. Air rushes around me as I go airborne. I land with a thud that jars my bones. Coughing, I spit black blood onto the ground. I sense the next hit coming and roll out of the way, barely missing the heel strike that was aimed at my back. Why is this creature even bothering? I thought he would have given up by now. I'm not worth this trouble.

We dip and dodge until my breath starts to labor. With a burst of speed, I somehow land near enough to swipe my fingers over the nepha's ankle before he flaps a few strides away. Was it enough?

The nepha looks down at his ankle with a frown. Are my secretions working? As if he stepped in hellhound shit, he shakes his foot. I have to move. Now. I just hope my drugs have distracted him enough. I sprint so fast, a little burst of noise sounds behind me as I displace the air. My magic flares stronger into my eyes.

I grin as the nepha's head starts to lift. *Yes! Just one look. Give me your eyes. Just one little look ...*

The monster smiles, hiding his eyes behind his wing, and a chuckle lilts from his lips. Damn it.

A ridiculous idea slips through my mind. Before I can talk myself out of it, I gather what little magic I have left. I keep my eyes on the nepha's face, just in case I'm able to catch his eyes as I say, "You may be stronger, but I'm faster."

He scoffs, crossing his arms. "I don't thin—"

Flooding my body with my magic, moving so fast little tingles of electricity lick over my skin, I run away. Straining, I listen for the sounds of pursuit. *Come on. Come get me, you cocky bastard.* A small smile lifts my lips as the sound of furiously flapping wings comes from behind me. *Okay. Please, let this work.*

A heartbeat before the nepha reaches me, I stop. It's so abrupt, it feels like my brain slams against the front of my skull. But it worked. He can't stop in time, and I simply turn and jump, wrapping my arms around his neck. He growls, his wide eyes almost meeting mine. Damn it. So close!

The nepha spears into the sky, and I cling to him. Just touching the strong monster allows me to siphon some of his plentiful magic. I grin, even as his wing tips stab into my back between his frantic flapping to keep us off the ground.

The nepha grabs me as he says, "Get off me you little pest."

"No. You were right. I need your magic." I chuckle through the pain of his feathers stabbing me again as I wrap my legs around his waist. I press as much of my drug-slick skin against his naked body, grateful I'm not wearing my kilt.

The erratic flapping and stabbing of the monster's wings works in my favor. He pitches to the side, and we start to fall. Sweat glistens on his gold-dusted skin, making him look even more celestial.

He's trying to fight against the drugs, but the ground is closing in fast. New cuts open on my palm as I rip a feather from the nepha's wing. My claws can't penetrate this creature's skin, but his feathers can. Stabbing the point deep into his chest, I rip a deep gash. Luck, or maybe the fates, are with me this turn. My mouth waters as the nepha's gold blood pours from the wound. Greedily, I lick and suck, consuming as much magic as I can before we hit the ground. I'm able to take a few more swallows, healing all but the deepest of my wounds before I'm ready to jump free to avoid being crushed. I eye the ground, picking a place to land, and with a little kick against his stomach, I fly backwards, tumbling in a flip before landing on my feet like a cat.

The nepha's body lands hard, a cloud of dust billowing up around him on impact. Groaning, he turns his head towards me. He keeps his eyes closed as he chokes out, "Damn you." He pushes to brace himself on his forearm, but he sways, his head lolling from the drugs coursing through him.

I don't waste time. In a blink, I'm kneeling next to him. I slap a hand to his thigh, pushing more of my hallucinogenic secretions into his skin. He groans, falling on his back, and he starts to get hard. Well, it looks like this nepha will die with a smile on his face.

I could really make a feast of this, consume this monster slowly, enjoy every bite. But I go for the power. Ripping the gold feather from his chest, I use it to deepen the wound. Wet ripping sounds surround me as I dig for his heart. The entire time, his smile stays in place, but his body twitches with each deep slice, and the pulled, pinched expression around his closed eyes gets deeper. Reaching between muscle and ribs, I wrap my hand around his heart and pull. It resists, but finally, the organ snaps free. Six bites is all it takes for me to completely consume the nepha's heart and all the hot, golden blood.

Almost immediately, the heart starts to reform in their open chest. These fuckers are really hard to kill. I wonder if Max knows how. Not that I'd ever want him to try. No. No one messes with the nepha unless they are truly desperate.

Sitting back on my heels, I lift my head to the dark sky. My body vibrates with magic. The stars look like they're pulsing. The colors of the trees, the grass, even the dirt, is more vivid. I feel *everything*. The rush of power is almost painful. My skin feels too tight. I take a slow breath, letting the magic settle. When I'm a bit calmer, I glance back at the nepha. Can I handle more? Just seeing his gold blood leaking onto his skin and dripping onto the ground is too tempting. There's so much power here. I shouldn't waste it.

Just a little more. I have to be quick. A downed nepha

will draw other monsters, and the last thing I want to do is get embroiled in another battle. Leaning over, I use the nepha's feather to slice the newly, half-formed heart from his chest. It's more tender, nearly melting in my mouth like ambrosia. I'm slightly dizzy from the magic.

I go back for more, but then freeze as a sudden wave of magic flares behind me. A deep voice with a resonance that seems to vibrate against my bones says, "Impressive work, Vex. But I think you've had enough."

A bolt of bronze light spears past me, slamming into the nepha on the ground. His skin starts to turn grey, then flakes and peels away. In just a matter of moments, the monster is nothing but ash, then that blows away, leaving nothing of the nepha I just took down. The beam of light winks out.

Unable to keep the tremble from my hands, I turn slowly to face yet another nepha.

Malicious.

My heart sinks to my stomach. I know this monster. Everyone knows Malicious. He is even more beautiful, with bronze skin and wings. The metallic shine of his feathers ends in black tips, matching his shiny black hair that's unbound, floating around him with a magical breeze. A bronze laurel headband sits in his dark locks, and while it should look ostentatious, the adornment just makes him look more ethereal.

His silver eyes hold amusement, and my body goes cold with fear. While Nepha are at the top of the monster hierarchy, Malicious is at the top of the nepha.

And I just took the magic of one of his kind.

I need to run.

A hand grips my hair. I didn't see him move. Shit. Reaching back, I wrap my hand around his wrist. With the other nepha's magic coursing through me, it won't be long until even the great Malicious collapses from the contact with my drugged skin.

My eyes widen as he tugs me back, the front side of his rock-hard body nearly knocking the breath from my lungs. He licks my face, then chuckles. "Good try, Vex."

When I tighten my grip on his arm, I realize his skin is even harder than the other nepha's was. In fact, it feels like I'm holding onto stone. My secretions aren't penetrating. *Shit. Shit. Shit. What do I do? How …? Fates save me. Max. I need …*

Malicious flaps his wings, and a sob bubbles from my throat as I brace for death, so much regret weighing on my soul. But then his arm wraps around me, and my feet lift off the ground. I'm airborne once again. His fingers in my hair grip tighter as he pulls my head back. We rise higher as Malicious' deadly calm voice rumbles over the rush of air. "You're coming with me, Vex."

CHAPTER 12

MAX

It's been three days. I've barely slept since that night with Vex. Fuck. Vex. I really messed up.

I didn't mean to fall asleep that night, but I was so tired from being up for almost forty hours. And then the sex. Fuck, *the sex.* I meant to take care of Vex. They responded so well to me. They were so beautiful as they fell apart on my lap. When I woke with them still on top of me, it took me a moment to remember where I was. Realizing I failed to see to Vex's comfort, the words burst from my mouth, "*I shouldn't have—*" And then Vex was gone.

I've tried to convince myself it wasn't hurt in their eyes I saw before The Divide ripped them from my arms. But of course Vex would assume I regretted what happened between us, why wouldn't they? The way I've acted toward them ...

But that's not the case. I was about to say, "*I shouldn't have fallen asleep. I'm sorry.*"

And now, they're gone.

That first night, I stayed up, kitchen door wide open, standing within the wards I can only assume are still in place around my house. I thought about re-blooding my threshold, but I didn't. I wanted Vex to be able to come right inside as soon as they showed up. But The Divide fell, and they didn't come. And the night after, and again, last night, nothing.

I glance at my kitchen table, the ache in my chest spreading at the sight of the items sitting there. Vex has left me, just like everyone else, but I can't leave things as they are. I won't live with any more 'what-if's.'

I won't.

I hate miscommunication. While I can't be sure how Vex took my last words to them, I need to explain. If something else has changed, if they don't want me, then ... I'll survive. I'll be okay, eventually. Maybe. But this isn't about me.

The click of the magazine sliding into my gun is loud and satisfying. I holster the pistol at my thigh. My second gun is already in place on my belt, along with two knives and extra magazines. I pat the plates of my body armor sitting heavy over my chest. Leaning down, I grab my rifle, slinging it over my head crossbody. Securing the weight of the weapon against my back, I tug the sling strap tight.

Wiggling my toes in my boots, I let the anticipation of the impending hunt thrum through me. I slip my custom ear plugs in place. They were designed for the military. Normal sound gets through just fine, so I'll be aware of my surroundings, but anything over a certain decibel—like when I fire my gun—the noise canceling kicks in, protecting my hearing.

I move to stand before my open kitchen door. Rolling my shoulders, I crack my knuckles. Vex still isn't out there. The Divide went down several hours ago, so I only have a few hours left to wait until it goes back up.

With determination straightening my spine, I stride out into the night. My boots strike the pavement, the sound echoing softly down the empty street. When I reach the end of the row of houses without encountering anything, I turn, heading towards the main street. I stop in the center of the empty road, the edges of two street lights crossing over me, spotlighting my position. I grab the hilt of my knife, and the blade slides silently from its sheath. With a quick slice, I cut my arm. As my blood starts to well, I switch my knife to my other hand and slide my pistol out of its holster. Raising my arm, I fire into the sky. The scent of gunpowder wafts up my nose, and I lower my arm.

I wait.

It doesn't take long for a clicking sound to come from behind me. I turn slowly, facing the spider-like monster rounding a corner. The razor-sharp ends of its many legs scrape and screech against the pavement. Green goo drips from its fangs as it lifts its head, sniffing the air. This one, despite its many eyes, can't see well. It relies on sound vibrations against its sensitive skin as well as scent. I haven't personally killed this type of monster, but I know how. Like ninety percent of monsters, decapitation will work just fine. This one also has a vulnerable spot on its under belly that'll drop it real quick.

At least it's not one of those angel monsters. There's a big rule amongst hunters ... You see an angel, you run. No one survives an attack from an angel.

I stay absolutely still, barely breathing. Adrenaline and hope are the only things keeping me upright. I need more sleep. I did try, but every time I closed my eyes, all I saw was Vex's hurt expression as The Divide pulled them away from me. That, or their face lit up in ecstasy as they came around my cock. Neither memory allowed me to fall into sleep.

My muscles bunch as the spider monster gets closer. And closer.

Its head snaps in my direction, and I realize my blood has trickled down my arm and a drop of it just splattered on the street. I didn't hear it, but the monster did. It lifts its head again, sniffing, the little hairs all over its body standing on end.

Come on, you fucker. Just a little closer.

A growl comes from my left. Then another. And another. Swiveling at my waist, I try to keep one eye on the spider monster as I look towards the growls. Hellhounds. At least three of them. Their eyes glow at me from the shadows, and the lead hound steps out into the street. It lowers its head, its lips pulled back, baring its teeth. Its hackles are raised, and its barbed tail thrashes behind it.

Okay. Not great.

The spider monster has stopped, its head swaying side to side as it tries to pick up the sounds and scents of the newcomers. Slowly, I raise my arm, aiming my pistol, holding the textured hilt of the knife in my other hand at my side. The hellhounds are easier to kill, though when they work in packs, it's a little harder. Still, I'll have to take down the hellhounds so I can focus on killing the spider. Scenarios—issues and solutions—run through my mind. I picture different attacks and how I will counter them.

On a slow exhale, I make eye contact with the lead hound. Its growl deepens, then it releases a gravely bark.

I've fired twice before the hound has even closed half the space between us. The second round hits its shoulder, and it yelps, stumbling. I fire again, nailing the second hellhound right in the eye. It goes down without a sound, skidding a few feet before stopping, dead. The third one sprints forward, the lead hound limping behind. Before I can shoot again, the fast click-clack of the spider's legs draws closer.

I spin just in time to fall backwards, narrowly avoiding the swipe of one long, spindly leg. My entire weight lands on my rifle, and I swear. I hope the sight isn't damaged. The third hound leaps. From my position on the ground, I raise my pistol and fire. The bullet slams into its chest just as one of the spider's other legs spears it through the neck.

I scramble out from under the spider as it skitters and shakes, trying to dislodge the dead hellhound. A grunt of pain rips from me as the lead hound sinks its teeth into my calf. The muscle is already going numb, and the puncture marks burn. The hellhound shakes its head, and it feels like my leg is about to rip clean off. I scream as I stab at the hound, aiming for its neck, but with all the thrashing, I miss and slice into its shoulder. It growls, its jaws tightening. I'm surprised my bone hasn't been crushed into pieces yet.

I twist, pressing the barrel of my pistol right to the hound's head, but before I can pull the trigger, agony sears my entire right side, and my gun falls from my hand, my paralyzed arm hanging limp. The spider looms over me with the hellhound still tearing at my leg. Green, venomous saliva drips from the spider's fangs, and I roll, hound and all, to keep more of the substance from landing on me.

The hellhound finally releases my leg, but immediately lunges, this time coming for my now exposed stomach. At the same time, the spider rears back, raising four of its deadly legs with a loud screech, and sticky webbing flies towards me.

Fuck.

There's a grunt, yip, then crunch. From the corner of my eye, I see wings and horns—blue horns with a silver cuff on one of them. I don't have time to worry about yet another monster joining the fight. Some of the spider's webbing has stuck one of my boots to the pavement. Leaning down with a quick slice of my blade, I work myself free. Pain erupts down my back, and the air punches from my lunges as I fly forward. The spider follows its strike, scrambling on its spindly legs to pin me down.

With my one good arm, I loosen my sling. As I roll over, I awkwardly rotate my rifle around my body and fire a burst of rounds into the spider's belly. The monster screams so loud, it activates my ear plugs. Venomous blood pours from its wounds. There's no avoiding it. I brace for the burn, catching another flash of blue wings before I raise my arm to try to shield my face.

CHAPTER 1[illegible]

VEX

I've been running at full speed for a while. A scowl pulls at my face. Why couldn't Malicious have brought me back home? Asshole.

That damned nepha kept me locked in a room so tightly warded, it was hard to breathe. At first, I had no idea why he brought me to the dark castle in the mountains. I spent that first turn alone and waiting for The Divide to fall. Once it did, I found I couldn't pass through to the human realm. I was thoroughly trapped, unable to get back to Max. I spent the entire six hours pacing and swearing and punching the walls. To no avail. Then the next turn, Malicious showed up with his cold, wicked smile in place. I expected a lot of things ... pain, torture, death. But he just asked me a single question.

"How did you find your mate?"

I was so stunned, I just gaped at him for a long moment. The smallest twitch of his bronze wings snapped me out of it fast enough. I told him it was truly fate. He sneered, asking the question again. I could only respond with the same answer. But it wasn't what he wanted to hear.

Over and over, he asked. And each time I said the same thing. I said it calmly, I screamed it at him. I asked him why he cared so much. I demanded he let me go. I even tried to attack him once, but that ended with me slumped against a wall with a burn mark searing my thigh from one of his light-blasts. Finally, I just stopped responding. Three turns passed with Malicious coming and going from the dark room, never saying or asking anything other than that one question. I would have felt bad for the nepha, but he was keeping me from my mate, and it was slowly driving me mad.

Then, an hour or so ago, several hours after The Divide fell, Malicious waved a hand. An opening appeared in one of the walls, and he nodded. "Go."

I had no idea why Malicious was letting me go, but without a moment's hesitation, I bolted into the perpetual night and ran. I kept my senses alert to see if the powerful nepha was following me, but I didn't sense him. That doesn't mean he won't show up unexpectedly at some point. But maybe, maybe he found what he was looking for.

The Divide is about to go back up. I need to see Max, to explain why I've been away, to apologize. There's so much magic thrumming through me, I'm barely putting any effort into my frantic speed as I race through the night.

After what feels like an eternity, my house comes into view. I blast through my gardens and onto the gravely back path. I skid to a stop, my feet scraping against the tiny stones. I don't feel it. All I feel is the driving need to get back to my mate. There's not much time before The Divide goes back up, but I can feel Max just on the other side. It's Valentine's Day. And my mate is alone. Tears prick my eyes. Is he angry? Anxious? Has he been looking for me to show up each night outside his house? Or is he ... glad I haven't come back?

I glance towards the door that leads to my kitchen with the urge to go grab my kilt. After those last words from Max, I don't know if he'd appreciate me showing up suddenly after my three-day absence, not to mention stark naked.

Clenching my hands, I tell myself to stop wasting time. I reach for the magic of The Divide and push. It's like hitting a frozen wall of ice. I can't get through to the human realm. I'm too late. The Divide is back up.

"Noooo."

Now I have to wait another full turn to get back to Max. Tears burn my eyes, and my shoulders slump. Fucking Malicious. I'd kill him if I could. But at this point, I'd be happy to never see the nepha ever again.

A crash sounds from inside my house. With blurring speed, I slam into my kitchen, the door blowing off its hinges. With a flick of my hand, all the light obs flare to life throughout my house, chasing away any shadows for the intruder to hide in.

But how did someone get in past my wards?

I stand still, sensing, listening.

A familiar groan meets my ears, and a surprised sob bursts from my chest as I rush to my living area. Sliding to a stop, my feet squeaking on the polished stone floor, I gasp. "Max!"

He grunts from where he's sitting on the floor, knees pulled up to his chest. In his arms, he's holding something, but I can't see what. All I see is the blood. It's everywhere.

He's covered in it. And from the smell, it's his. I also smell venom. What the hell happened? I fall to my knees at his side, lightly running my fingers over his shoulder. "Max. What are you ..? How are you ...? Here, let me heal you." It's hard to tell through all the blood where the actual wounds are, so I just start touching him all over. He's shaking, but he's warm, and he's here. I work my way over his arms, one of which hangs limp, cradled between his thighs and chest. My hands move across his torn shirt over his back. I try to reach between his hunched body and his knees, but he doesn't budge, clinging tightly to whatever he's holding against his chest. I don't push, moving my hands to the fabric of his pants, sending my magic over his hips and thighs. Skin to skin is better for my healing, but I don't ask him to remove his clothes. He hasn't said a word, and his silence is killing me.

After I've touched all of him that I can, I sit back, crossing my legs. I lean in, resting my hand in the crook of his arm. "Max?"

He takes a slow breath, then finally lifts his head just a little so I'm able to see what he's holding. A ... little potted rose bush? When I lift my gaze to his face, all I see are the tears in his eyes and a bruise on his cheek. With my heart in my throat, I run my fingers over his face, caressing softly. The discoloration of his skin fades, and the swelling goes down. I keep touching him. I can't stop.

Finally, he breaks the silence. "I drank spider blood."

My brows furrow. "What?"

"You know those spider-looking monsters with the blades for legs? I drank its blood. I—"

"Wait, you killed a menace?"

His voice is low and throaty. "That what they're called? Not exactly. There were hellhounds too, and well ... things were not going well." My heart is in my stomach, and I want to shake him and scream at him never to do something like that again. But I hold my tongue as he goes on. "Then this giant gargoyle looking monster came flying in and killed the final hound before ripping the menace thing apart. He helped me collect the blood I needed and got me back to my house. Said his name was Paine, and that if we ever needed anything to come to the blue townhouse across the street. I knew something was going on over there."

I take a slow breath of relief. "Yeah, I know Paine. He found his mate over Christmas. He's a decent monster, but you wouldn't want to get on his bad side."

Max chuckles. "Yeah, I got that from all the maiming and killing. He didn't even break a sweat." Max jolts. "Shit. He gave me something. Said to give it to you. Something about an ancient and a bond. I didn't really understand. I was in a lot of pain."

I blink, reaching for the crumpled paper Max pulls from his pocket. Unfolding it with shaking hands, I read the neat handwriting. I read it again, just to be sure. There's a way to break the magic of The Divide. A true bond between mates. A claiming bite. Holy shit. Seems I owe Paine a great debt—one I don't think I'll ever be able to repay. I'll have to thank him next time I'm in the human realm.

Max shifts, raising his arm, pressing his hand over mine where it's gripping the note. I relax my grip, shaking my head as I say, "I'll tell you later." He closes his eyes with a nod, and some of my panic comes out as I ask, "Why were you outside at night, Max?"

His eyes pinch tighter before releasing a slow exhale. He keeps his eyes closed, but says, "I needed that blood, no matter the cost. I had to find you." His eyes slowly open, and the raw emotion there nearly stops my heart. "I needed you to know. I ... Vex, that night, I got cut off. I know you probably thought I was ... Vex, what happened between us that night was special to me. I've thought of nothing else since. You have consumed my thoughts, my body, my ...

Heart? Please say I have your heart.

He clears his throat. "When I woke up, I realized I hadn't taken care of you properly. It couldn't have been comfortable for you to sleep like that. I'm sorry, Vex. I was in the middle of saying that I shouldn't have fallen asleep without cleaning us both up and tucking you into my bed." His voice rises slightly, panic lacing through his words. His eyes go hazy like he's no longer seeing me, but something in his past. "I needed you to know. I needed you to understand. Please, please don't ... I can't handle ... I told myself I'd accept it if you walked away, but I ... Please, please ..."

He clutches the little plant tighter, his shoulders hunching. My poor, loving mate. Max feels down to his soul, and he's been burned by love in the past. Of course he's terrified to face those flames once more.

My hands frame his face, the scruff of his facial hair scrapping my skin. I force him to look at me so he sees, so he understands. "Max. I will not leave you. Nothing will take me from you—not anything you do or say, not even death."

His watery eyes search mine. "But you did. You left. Three days, Vex."

The shame of failing my mate has me almost dropping my gaze, but I keep my eyes on him. "I wanted to return to you. I tried. But you're right. I failed you. I took on monsters I had no business challenging. I took one down, but another showed up. I should be dead, but he—"

Max grabs my hand. "Are you okay?"

I nod. "I am now. I really did want to come back to you, but that asshole nepha—"

"Nepha? As in Nephilim? Angels? One of those angel monsters?" I nod again and Max's eyes turn hard. "Vex. No. They are too powerful. Are you telling me you survived two angels?"

"Nepha, but ... yeah, I guess, but only because Malicious didn't want my magic. He wanted information." Max keeps staring at me, his blue eyes still shiny with the last of his tears. "He wanted to know how I found my mate. How I found you."

"What did you tell him?"

"That it was really, truly fate. He didn't believe me, or maybe he thought there was more to the story. I couldn't escape him."

"So, how are you here right now?"

"He let me go."

"Just like that?"

I pull our faces closer together. "Even if he hadn't, I would have found a way. I would have come back to you, Max. I'm a monster. I'll do unspeakable things just to be by your side."

He whimpers a broken sound, the sound of someone who has lost everything before. He has yet to talk about Reece's story, but I hope someday he'll open up about him. That pain, that fear of having the one you love ripped away from you ... it fills his eyes and leaks from his heart.

Making sure he's still looking into my eyes, I say, "You are not alone. I will not leave you. Ever."

He chokes out my name on a little exhale, and I meet him in the middle of what little distance there is between us. I thread my fingers through his hair, holding him as I kiss him. We both sigh as our lips brush and hold, needing that connection.

Max pulls back, pressing his forehead to mine. "Thank you, Vex." I kiss his nose, then he shifts again, glancing down, raising a brow. "No kilt?"

My cheeks flame as I shrug. "It was dirty, so I cleaned it and left it to dry. There wasn't time to put it back on. A human crashed into my house unexpectedly."

Max smiles, and my heart melts. Unfurling, he grabs the little pot, frowning as a few thorns stick to his shirt, and some red petals flutter to the floor. "I wasn't sure if this would make it through with me. It's in sorry shape, but it made it."

I smile at the little rose bush in Max's large hand. "Hey, it's the little wins."

His wide eyes snap to mine. His mouth drops open, then he asks on a whisper, "What did you just say?"

"It's the little wins. Your plant made it. Sure, it's not—"

His chuckle cuts me off. His free hand runs through his hair as he sighs. I'm not sure why those words affected him like this, but he's smiling. Another little win.

His grin widens as he holds out the pot towards me. My brows pinch. "For me?"

Max nods, and I take the pot, the little buds and blooms looking up at me. It's the perfect size to sit in my kitchen window. I'll put a sunlight orb right over it. The red flowers will brighten the room, and their scent will greet me each time I use the sink that sits under that window.

Max shifts, bringing my attention back to him. He reaches into his pocket, then holds up a little black velvet box. I stare at it, my pulse racing as he snaps the lid open.

Nestled inside the satin lining is a gold ear cuff with little obsidian gems sprinkled around it like tiny black stars.

I swallow the lump of emotions in my throat. "It's beautiful."

With his free hand, he runs his fingertips over the shell of my ear, and I shiver as he whispers, "So are you. So beautiful." And then he grins and says something that sends my heart soaring to the heavens. "Will you be my Valentine?"

CHAPTER 14

MAX

That beautiful glow erupts across their skin until they're shining like the brightest night sky. I don't think I've seen anything more glorious than my mate's beaming smile. Vex falls into my lap, hugging me, and I wrap an arm around them with a chuckle. "Is that a yes?"

They sit back, their smile impossibly larger. "Yes!" Their eyes fall to the open box. "Will you put it on me?"

With pleasure.

Now that Vex has healed me, my body is primed and buzzing with desire. The ear cuff feels small and delicate in my hand, just like Vex.

Two days ago, I needed to keep myself busy before I tore my hair out with worry, so I went into town. I usually work from home, running my identity protection business, but I like to meet new clients personally if they are local. People are all too willing to share every little thing about themselves online. And when those people end up in hot water, they call me. I handle cases from cyber stalking to identity theft and more. It pays well, and I enjoy the satisfaction of helping people.

On my way home from the new client's place, I saw the ear cuff in the window of a shop, and I knew that it was made for my mate. As I slip the gold piece over the edge of their ear, the little black gems wink at me, complimenting their starlight skin. I run my finger over the gold, then down their ear. They shudder under my touch, and I whisper, "Perfect."

A little frown pulls at their lips. "I didn't get you anything."

I caress their ear again with a feather-light touch as I let my gaze travel down their toned, naked body. "I have something in mind."

We reach for each other at the same time. Vex helps me take off my tattered shirt, and I quickly unfasten my pants, kicking them off with my boots. Once I'm naked, I wrap my arms around Vex and stand. I carry them bridal style into the grand hall off what I assume is the front door. I look around and growl impatiently. "I don't exactly remember from the last time I was here. Where's your bedroom?"

Vex hugs my neck, kissing my chest as they whisper, "Upstairs to the left. Third door on the left."

I bolt for the wide, curving stairs, taking them two at a time. "What the fuck do you do with all this space?"

They laugh. "I don't like to feel cramped. You don't like it?"

We reach the second floor, and I nearly run down the hall with a wicked grin. "You know what? I do. So many rooms to fuck you in, mate."

Their cock twitches against their stomach. Seems they like me calling them mate as much as I like saying it.

I barely pause in front of the third door, opening it quickly and carrying Vex into the already well-lit room. It's amazing how much has happened since the last time I was here. My bare feet dig into the plush rugs. My gaze lands on my dried blood near the bed. Vex notices, and with a wave of their hand, the stain is gone. I blink at them, holding them closer against my chest.

Vex smiles. "That nepha was very powerful. I'm overflowing with magic."

I nip their lips, then lick their ear until my teeth click against the gold cuff. "Good." From my peripheral, I see their toes curl as they rub their feet together. Slowly lowering them to the bed, I crawl over them, bracing my hands on either side of their head. "Thank you, Vex, for the light. I don't ... I don't like the dark."

Vex places their warm palm on my face, and that simple touch calms me as they ask, "Do you want to talk about it?"

I do. I want to tell Vex everything about Reece, how he lived so full of excitement and joy. How we fell in love. How we lived happily for so many years. And yes, I want Vex to know the specifics of how Reece died. I want to share the joy and pain of that part of my life because I know Vex will listen. Because I know I'm safe with Vex.

But I shake my head and lean down, brushing a kiss against their lips. "Not now. Later. Right now, I need you, Vex. We both almost died trying to get back to each other, and I need ..."

They reach for me, stroking my cock until I'm leaking pre-cum onto their stomach. "Yes, Max. Please." They roll their hips, and I grab their length, stroking in time with their pumping fist on me. A warm liquid suddenly covers their palm and cock. I groan, gritting my teeth. They stroke their warm lubricant all over my dick and balls as the lube also coats their length, making my pumps smoother.

Our breaths grow into pants, and my body tingles with the sparking pleasure spreading rapidly. I press a kiss to Vex's neck. "I need to taste you."

They buck into my hand with a beautiful moan, and I work my way down their body. Nipping and licking every inch of skin I come into contact with, I finally reach their cock. I nuzzle into the smooth skin at the apex of their thighs, then grin up at my writhing mate. "Grab hold, Vex. I want you to show me how you like it."

Keeping their eyes on me, their lips part. They reach for my head, pausing, and I nod. Their fingers scrape against my scalp, and I hum with pleasure. Vex grabs my hair, tugging slightly, and my gaze snaps back to their face. There's a moment when I swear I can hear our heart beats syncing, then Vex pushes my head down. We both groan as I wrap my lips around them, sucking them deep. Their rich, chocolate scent mixes with their salty taste. Vex is truly like a decadent dessert. The lube secreting from their skin doesn't really have a taste. It just tingles slightly on my lips and tongue. Those tingles intensify and soon, I feel like I'm floating in a pool of bliss and desire.

Vex guides my head, his cock hitting the back of my throat with each thrust of his hips. I relax and swallow him, taking my monster deeper and deeper. I'm really getting into it, when Vex yanks me off them and pulls me upwards. Obediently, I crawl up their body until we're face to face. My fingers find the gold cuff again, tracing the delicate piece of jewelry. Vex's mouth parts on a silent moan, and they lean into my caress.

I nip their lips. "What does my mate want?" They shift, bending their legs until their knees are on either side of their waist, spread open for me. I hum. "Yes. So beautiful."

"This feels like a dream."

My body presses flush with theirs as I kiss them. It does feel like a dream, but I'm not going to say it's too good to be true. I'm going to take this gift from the fates or whoever or whatever brought Vex into my life. I'm going to take my mate and never let go.

Rolling my hips, I give in to the pleasure. My shimmering monster presses their head into the bed, arching their back. I can't help myself. Leaning down, I lick then bite one peaked nipple. They hiss, and I suck it into my mouth, rolling the nub over my tongue. Their hands find my hair again, and they pull as they plead, "Please, Max."

I shift back. Their entrance clenches in anticipation, their hole dripping with their lube. I'm like a broken record, but they really are just so beautiful. Lining myself up, I roll my hips, letting the tip of my cock ease past their tight rim. I take in everything, their sparkling glowing skin, their panting breaths, their midnight hair, the flex of their muscles, the wink of the gold cuff ...

Vex plants their feet on the bed and bucks up, slamming my cock inside them. I groan, but the sound that comes from Vex is a deep growl that nearly has me coming. With their strength, my little mate grips my hips and holds me in place as they fuck themselves on me from the bottom.

"Jesus, Vex. Yes, just like that." They growl again, and my balls tighten. "Fuck. I'm so close. I wanted this to last, but—"

Vex does something with their hips, and at the same time they grip their cock. "Not, yet, Max. Say it again. I want to hear it." They punch their hips up again, but this time they stop and hold still. My cock throbs inside them, and my orgasm is so close to the edge, my body is shaking. I'm trying to hold back, but the pleasure is clawing at me. I try to pump my hips for that last bit of friction that will send me over, but Vex's hold is like a vice. My monster has taken control. They hook their heel over my calf, saying again. "Say it, Max. Say it and come with me."

I know what they want. And I want it too. I look deep into Vex's eyes, absorbing this moment. I can't hold back anymore. I nod, and Vex loosens their grip just enough so I can finally pull my hips back. I thrust into Vex with a shout as I come. "My mate!"

Their growls deepen and get louder, prolonging my orgasm. I'm lost in the starry shimmer of Vex's skin, my body breaking apart in bliss. I watch with eagerness as their hand pumps furiously along their cock. My orgasm continues to scrape and pull at my lower belly, and I thrust once more, hitting that sensitive spot inside them. Vex shouts as thick ropes of cum splash over their chest and stomach.

I want to collapse on the bed and pull them to me, but I won't chance falling asleep again. Instead, I gaze at my mate as they come down from their climax, their breathing slowly evening out, their skin still glowing softly. I kiss their cheek, their nose, their forehead. Brushing their soft midnight hair of out their eyes, I ask, "What does the glowing really mean?"

They hold my gaze for a moment before they say, "Anza glow when they're ... when they're in love."

I nuzzle into Vex's neck with a hum. "Mmm. I like that. You're my own little love nightlight, chasing away the darkness."

They sigh, relaxing against me. Vex really is perfect for me.

I lift my limp mate into my arms, and my cum leaks

out of their ass. I kiss the top of their head, breathing in that vanilla and chocolate scent, now tinged with the steamy scent of sex. As I walk towards the bathroom, I close my teeth around the gold ear cuff, enjoying the little gasp that comes from their lips. With a whisper against their ear, I say, "Thank you for not giving up. Thank you for stalking me." They chuckle, and I burrow my nose deeper in their hair as I whisper, "Happy Valentine's Day, mate."

Vex squirms, using their strength to cling to me like a monkey. Before I know it, they have their legs wrapped around my waist, their chest pressed to mine, their arms around my neck. They smile the most beautiful smile I've ever seen, completely stealing my heart as they say, "I'll never give up on you. I quite enjoy stalking your sexy ass. Happy Valentine's Day, mate."

THE END

The monsters of The Divide will continue with Malicious the nepha's story for a fun summer read. Coming summer 2024.

ALSO BY T. B. WIESE

I genuinely hope you enjoyed this series. If you're interested, here are my other books - all adult fantasy with varying levels of spice.

Scan the code below for links to my Amazon author page where you'll find all my other books.

You'll also find a link to my website for signed paperbacks & hardcovers as well as swag.

ACKNOWLEDGMENTS

A huge thank you to my readers. Without you, this crazy dream of being an author would not be possible.

To all my beta & ARC readers, thank you! You had a big hand in making this series what it is today. Thank you so very much for taking the time to help me polish this story.

And lastly, I want to thank all my friends and family for cheering me on and being as excited about my characters as I am—I love my tribe.

ABOUT THE AUTHOR

T. B. Wiese is a military spouse, dog mom, photographer, Disney nerd, and lover of spicy fantasy. She loves animals (She grew up with dogs and working with horses, including working at the Tri-Circle D Ranch at Disney World), so don't be surprised when you find yourself reading lovable animal characters in her novels.

If you'd like to keep up to date with future releases as well as new swag and sales, sign up for her newsletter via link in code below.

SCAN THE CODE WITH YOUR CAMERA APP
FOR HER SOCIAL LINKS

Made in United States
North Haven, CT
03 February 2024